Passenger to Nowhere

by Anthony Gilbert

Sarah Hollis, a young English girl with a broken romance, rents a villa in the French Alps with two friends. Arriving a week ahead of the other girls, she finds herself alone in a sinister, ghostly house with a locked room, memories of an eccentric old woman now dead, and strong rumors of buried treasure.

Soon Sarah learns that her supposed landlady is an impostor, and the rightful owner's claims are being challenged by a good-looking American male of doubted origins. To her horror she discovers that someone is forcibly trying to remove her from the scene by tampering with her car. Though warned to leave the villa, she refuses. Then, suddenly, she disappears under violent conditions.

Meanwhile, in France on another case, the doughty Arthur Crook is pressed into service. Aided by the local curé—most delightful of priest-detectives since Father Brown—Crook lumbers his way into local police councils and uncovers a recent corpse shot in the back. Dashing about in his ancient yellow Rolls, he speedily links Sarah's disappearance to the murder and proceeds to foil the desperate plot into which she has stumbled. With his usual brusque charm, he even plays Cupid briefly as Sarah finds a more lasting love.

Recent Books by **Anthony Gilbert**

NO DUST IN THE ATTIC

RING FOR A NOOSE

THE FINGERPRINT

THE VOICE

PASSENGER TO NOWHERE

Passenger to
NOWHERE

PASSENGER TO *NOWHERE*

Anthony Gilbert

RANDOM HOUSE

New York

First American edition

Library of Congress Catalog Card Number: 66-11998

MANUFACTURED IN THE UNITED STATES OF AMERICA
by The Book Press, Brattleboro, Vt.

Passenger to *NOWHERE*

I

The little red car, bumping from stone to stone down a lane that, thought Sarah, in a more civilized country would have been marked Bullocks Only, rounded its final curve and stopped dead on the edge of a water-splash that looked about half as deep as a canal. The girl behind the wheel opened the windows, lighted a cigarette and, in the words of the hymn, "surveyed the landscape o'er." It had been one of those baking days with a sky like a caldron, and she had been driving south since breakfast.

I suppose, she reflected tolerantly, that French couple I met don't have the same vibrations as I do. I'd have sworn they said down this lane, but surely they might have warned me I had to swim the last part.

Swimming was one of the delights she anticipated in this holiday in the French Alps, but not across a road and not every time she wanted to leave the house. Except for herself the world seemed empty of human life. On her right an ancient wall rose forbiddingly, with a stiff frieze of dark poplars that would, she thought, have concealed a modern cathedral from the public view, let alone Abercrombie's Folly, the improbable name of the villa where she expected to spend the next four weeks. On her left the land was planted with vines, little stiff dark plants that one assumed would only yield the most vinegary of *vin ordinaire*. On her right was the wall; beyond the water-splash the road wound meaninglessly around another curve; and in the distance the sturdy white Charollais cattle cropped and drowsed, oblivious to anything so insignificant as a girl of twenty-three in a small red car, escaping from a ruptured heart.

It was only six weeks ago that Simon, to whom she had been engaged for a year, had discovered it was Susan Main, not Sarah Hollis, he wanted to marry—Susan, a big, dark girl so earnest she made you think of Mr. Oscar Wilde's play.

"So fortunate we discovered our mistake in time," said Simon.

"Your mistake," corrected Sarah.

"Divorce is so messy," amplified Simon. "And naturally once Susan and I had realized our feelings for each other, integrity would have made it imperative . . ."

"What a funny word to use!" Sarah suggested.

"You'll find someone who'll suit you much better that I'd ever have done," Simon labored on encouragingly.

"That shouldn't be difficult," said Sarah's bosom friend Pat. "Oh, Sarah, wake up and realize how lucky you are. It's like the time I couldn't go to Paris because I broke my arm and the train was wrecked and you can be sure I'd have been the one person to be killed."

"Pat's so right," agreed Polly, the third member of the St. John's Wood ménage. "Suet pudding may be lovely in the winter, though I can't stand the stuff myself, but for a daily diet all the year round . . ."

Sarah ungratefully couldn't feel in debt to Fate for making such a mess of her life; she found Mrs. Abercrombie's letter which said the villa would be empty if any of them wanted to come a week early, sent a telegram, managed to get a ticket for the Channel ferry and here she was, stuck two-thirds of the way down a more or less impenetrable lane—so far as she could tell, a passenger to nowhere.

It was very restful down in the valley. Some insects, cicadas or particularly enthusiastic bees—she couldn't decide which —were holding an indignation meeting of some sort close by. Otherwise there was no sound. Even the ubiquitous planes seemed to eschew this part of the world. She finished her cigarette and sat basking in the sun in the company of a lizard who preened himself on a nearby stone.

You would think, reflected Sarah again, that Abercrombie would be the same in any language.

She wondered what on earth had persuaded an Englishwoman to settle here in the first place.

Mrs. A. had sent lyrical photographs of the villa and even more lyrical letters, about strawberries, asparagus beds, mountain views, even a married couple, Martin and Marie, who would stay on and assist with the housekeeping.

"I wonder," Polly had mused—she was the lazy one—"if the service will include breakfast in bed."

"Strawberries," Pat had said dreamily. "I suppose Madame doesn't keep a cow."

Sarah put the car into gear, reversed with some difficulty and started the steep, upward climb. The villa, if it really existed, must be built on remarkably unequal levels—assuming, of course, she'd come the right way. When she reached the upper road it was as empty as the road to the villa had been. Under that enormous blue sky the world seemed asleep. Even the leaves on the trees hung motionless, and when she lighted a second cigarette the smoke went straight up into the air. The little car seemed to have absorbed more than its share of sun, so she alighted and sat on a bit of coping that enjoyed a few inches of shade. Far to her left she saw the mountains capped with snow; the road to the right led to the tiny village of St. Mariole. Coming through it half an hour ago she had thought this must be early closing day; there were only a few shops and they were all shut. I've come to the end of the world, she decided, but there were worse things than sitting here in this lovely landscape waiting for something to happen.

She had crossed from England the night before last and decided to break her 500-odd-mile journey into two parts—no sense wearing yourself out at the very beginning of a holiday—so she had spent last night at a little wayside hotel in a place whose name she didn't even recall. The tourist season didn't appear to touch this part of France, though since it was only early May, it might be fairer to say the season hadn't started. Anyhow, she'd been given accommodation at once and shown into a room no other country in Europe would have produced.

Already the excitement engendered by finding herself in new surroundings, breathing an unfamiliar air, seeing different advertisements, hearing a different tongue, had begun to exert its inevitable charm. She looked about her little chamber with a delight she wouldn't have displayed had she found herself in the new Hilton. The bed was high and covered with a flowered counterpane. There were more flowers on the twenty-year-old wallpaper. The basin and bidet were concealed behind a piece of someone's outworn dining-room curtains. Lying in bed she could trace shadows and shapes on the ceiling and listen to the gruff gurgle of water running through the rustry pipes.

There was no sitting room, of course, but there was a minute bar opening off the *salle à manger* and she turned in there to buy herself a drink. There was only one other occupant, a plump, square, ginger-colored person with a big red face, popping brown eyes, hair and brows the color of a fox, and a suit that must have been chosen to match them. The brightest I ever saw, she thought, ordering a vermouth and soda.

She nearly fell over with surprise when the stranger turned toward her and said, in a voice that could have been heard in the Straits of Dover, "Another limey as I live. Well, I said this 'ud be my lucky day." He beamed his approval of the shining fair hair, the charming, faintly tinted mouth, the little gold earrings shaped like bells that swung in her ears.

"O.K.," he said to the waiter, "you can put that down to me." He seemed to take it for granted that she was going to sit at his table, and seeing he'd paid for her drink she didn't seem to have much choice.

"Name of Crook," the stranger continued. "Arthur Crook of London."

"I come from London, too," she told him.

His brown eyes beamed on her. "On your own? Holiday? Or like me, earning your bread and jam in a foreign land?"

"I didn't know anyone paid a person to come to France," Sarah exclaimed.

"You wouldn't find me on the continong without someone hired me," Crook assured her. "Some chap from home who's having a difference of opinion with the police and thinks I might be able to find the missing link over here."

"I'm on holiday," said Sarah firmly. "A whole month and nothing to do but enjoy myself. I'm staying at a place called St. Mariole—I daresay you've never heard of it . . ."

"Too right I haven't. Finish that, sugar, and have the other half," he added, indicating her glass. "Staying with friends?"

"We've rented a villa, three of us—remote, restful and romantic, that's what the advertisement said."

"You want to watch out," he advised her cordially. "These frogs have their own ideas of romance."

"So had Simon," she told him, and stopped aghast. She wasn't a girl who opened her grief to all and sundry. Simon used to tell her she had a suspicious nature. Loving is giving, he said; it had all boiled down to the fact that he deplored her stinginess in refusing to go to bed with him before marriage. Presumably Susan was less inhibited.

Her companion took the name in his stride. "Simon the boy friend?"

"He—well, yes, I suppose you could say that. Was, rather," she added honestly.

"But you've thought better of it. Bully for you. I spend my

life telling my clients that if they'd thought a bit longer they wouldn't be in the jams they are. But in that case, of course, they wouldn't be needing my services. Fortunately there's a fool born every minute, so I'm never likely to be out of a job."

She cried incredulously, "Does that mean you're a lawyer? That is—I mean—"

"I know just what you mean, sugar, and I don't blame you a bit. You think of a lawyer as a natty chap with white slips to his waistcoat and a face like a balk of teak." He felt in his bright brown pocket and pulled out a card as big as an advertisement. "No, take it, I've plenty more. I know you don't think you'll ever want it, but then, I daresay a month ago you didn't expect to find yourself brightening my day."

"Arthur Crook, your trouble our business," she read. "Twenty-four-hour service." And two addresses, one in Bloomsbury, the other in Earl's Court.

"I know Earl's Court," she said impulsively. "When I first came to London I used to have a room in Redcliffe Gardens."

"Know The Two Chairmen?" he asked like a flash. "Well no, p'raps not, it's not a lady's pub. But the beer's good." He looked sadly at his own glass. "I've always had a notion the British come abroad for the pleasure of coming home again. Not, mind you," he added proudly, "that this is my first trip. I was over here in 1917 and it wasn't the Kaiser's fault I ever went back. Goodness knows, they did their best to stop me. Now, don't start doing arithmetic. My clock stopped at fifty-five, and I'm not proposin' to wind it up again."

"Is that your big yellow Rolls I saw in the garage?" asked Sarah, impressed.

"If that's what you call a garage. I suppose it belonged to cows once on a time. Now, sugar, not touting for custom, you understand—that's agin the law—but you put that card into your reticule, and if ever natural feeling gets the better of good sense and you're inclined to stick Simon with a paper-knife, just give me a tinkle when the bulls come along and . . ."

"Why on earth should you suppose I'd do anything so crazy?"

(9)

"Well, perhaps not Simon but the new Mrs. Simon," he agreed.

She realized that, with no help from her, he'd already sized up the situation.

" 'Why?' you ask. Well, you're female, aren't you? One nice thing about working for your sex is that a chap can't afford to shut his eyes or look the other way for a minute. And all the intuition in the world don't belong to women," he added, more severely.

"I didn't realize you'd brought your crystal ball along with you," said Sarah demurely.

"What I mean," pursued Mr. Crook, tireless as a lumbering bull that doesn't appear to make much pace but somehow gets to the fence before you, "is that there has to be some meaning in things, and why should you and me rub up against each other this particular evening in this particular pub? Say you walked into this villa of yours and found a corpse."

"But I shan't."

"Most likely not. I just said suppose you did. That's when you want an arrow or so in reserve, and I'm steel-tipped. Some people—the police for instance—say I'm poison-barbed as well, but you don't need me to tell you"—and he beamed like the rising sun—"you don't have to believe everything they say."

"I've got photographs," Sarah told him. "It's a villa, not a mausoleum."

"Where is it anyway?"

"It's in the French Alps, the Pyrenees, you know."

"All this map-changing," grumbled Mr. Crook. "Pyrenees meant Spain when I was a boy."

"This side of the Pyrenees, I mean. We saw the advertisement in the *Record,* so we wrote—we is the three of us, Polly and Pat and me—and it was available for a short time, so we took it."

"Just like that?" asked Mr. Crook. "I mean, you don't know anyone who's seen it?"

She rootled in her bag and produced a folder of pictures.

(10)

"Mrs. Abercrombie sent us these. She's the one who owns the villa. Look—the garden—mountain view—a corner of the villa—one of the rooms . . . We went to Alicante last year, and the noise—you wouldn't believe. Little railway running under your window—they were doing some work in a nearby quarry and they never seemed to stop, stalls put up about half past five, little yellow trams, horse carriages—and people talking all night. I can't think when the Spaniards go to bed."

"Sounds just my cup of tea," said Mr. Crook wistfully.

"So we thought, this year we won't make the same mistake. Just fancy waking up to see mountains. And the quiet!"

"You could say as much for the grave," said Crook, "but I never hankered to inherit my box before my time."

He looked at the photographs thoughtfully. Suddenly he said, "Ever hear tell of the House of Usher? A mansion of gloom, that's what the chap called it. Still, not to worry," he added in consoling tones, "I'm just an old London cabhorse. I like things cozy."

"You make things cozy," she told him involuntarily, and he turned with such an air of surprised delight she felt the color running up into her cheeks.

"I take that very kind, sugar. We aim to please—that's me and Bill Parsons. He's my assistant.

"I'm off at crack of dawn," he told her later, offering his enormous hand that could have crushed both of hers and hardly noticed what it was doing. "But just remember—any time—my pleasure."

"Are you going back to England?" she asked.

"Well, not right away. More's the pity. The trail leads me to Bordeaux, hotel called Collioure, if you should want to get in touch for any reason." He beamed like a genial buddha.

It was absurd, but the ache in her heart seemed a little less keen than before. It wasn't that the wound had miraculously healed, nothing like that, but she began to see for the first time since the break that there might be an end even to the end of the world.

Mr. Crook had gone when she came down next morning,

(11)

though she wasn't late; she lingered in the little paved court they called a garden, smoking a cigarette, then got back into the little red car and made tracks for the House of Usher.

Her reverie was interrupted by the sound of footsteps on the hard road, and she looked up to see a man and a woman who had presumably been to market, since *she* carried a pair of fowls, heads downward, and *he* had a crammed basket of food. Sarah wanted to leap up and rescue the fowls, then reminded herself she was only a visitor here, and perhaps French fowls got used to being carried upside down. She got up from her stone and walked toward the pair, who instantly regarded her with the most extreme suspicion. For a minute she thought they weren't even going to stop. Before she arrived here she had been regarded as the linguist of her group, but her French was like the fidelity of Cynara's lover, conforming to an individual pattern. In any case, even if they could have understood her, she would have been no better off, since they spoke in a patois as thick as one of their own soups. Nevertheless, she persisted. Abercrombie must be the same in every language, she reminded herself. At the mention of the name the woman became more animated but no more comprehensible. You couldn't say she was excited precisely; you certainly couldn't say she was helpful; but she threw up her arms, regardless of the plight of the unfortunate fowls, she shrugged her plump shoulders—even on this blazing day she wore a black coat and a black straw hat as if she were attending a funeral—and she talked remarkably fast.

"Villa Abercrombie," repeated Sarah in the loud voice people automatically employ to idiots and the deaf.

To her surprise the woman indicated the road from which she had just emerged. Sarah shook her head. "No way through," she insisted—"blind alley"—and tried to indicate by gestures that there was, perhaps, a further turning ahead. They might have gone on shaking and gesticulating, against a background of clucks from the fowls—the old man didn't speak, he was like someone deaf and perhaps he was—for the remainder of the evening, but for an unexpected intervention. A rusty bell suddenly rang out and a black apparition came sailing down the road looking like something out of an Arthur Rackham illustration. This was the parish priest, and his appearance seemed to set the seal on the whole unreal situation.

The newcomer turned to her. "You are looking for the villa?" He spoke English with an accent as rusty as his bicycle bell.

"I couldn't make them understand. I suppose my French . . ."

"I speak a little English, mademoiselle," he confided. "I was in the war, you understand." Sarah remembered hearing that Catholic priests fought in the ranks like anyone else, no privileges for them. "And I was a prisoner with some English soldiers for a year. 'Come and see us some time,' they said, when we were liberated." He smiled, showing teeth no larger than a five-barred gate. He had extraordinarily bright blue eyes set under a bony forehead; everything about him was large, big hard-working hands, big bones, an immense nose, bushy brows—for some reason she recalled the other stranger she had met who also had brows that nearly met above his nose.

"Unfortunately Madame has left," he went on.

When he understood that she and some friends, still in England, proposed to occupy the villa for a few weeks he looked incredulous.

"You have not seen the house, mademoiselle?"

"I've seen photographs, they look all right. Why, is it haunted or something?" She was remembering Mr. Crook's similar reaction to her news.

"Perhaps. I do not know. You are a friend of Madame's?"

"I never heard of her until we saw this advertisement. Doesn't she usually let it for the summer?"

"This is the first summer she has been in possession. The villa previously belonged to an old lady, a Miss Abercrombie, who died a few months ago. This Mrs. Abercrombie comes from Paris— she is not known to us here. At first no one could be sure . . ."

"Sure of what?"

"The identity of the rightful heir." He had taken his feet from the pedals and stood straddled over the ancient bicycle; there was a feeling of restfulness about him that seemed to suggest he had mastered time. He had plenty to spare for her and would still have enough for his other duties.

"Old Miss Abercrombie lived like a hermit, at home to no one, not even the priest. Of course, she was not a Catholic, yet she must have known it was I who would bury her at the last. The old lady had lived in great solitude since the death of her father. There had been a brother but he left long ago, before my time, you understand, mademoiselle. As a young priest I worked in the mission field."

"You mean, she lived here all alone in this desolate place?" Sarah sounded shocked. "Still, she had this couple, Martin and Marie. They're staying on—I suppose to see we don't do any damage. Did Mrs. Abercrombie inherit them with the villa?"

"There is some rumor that Madame intends to sell the villa, perhaps at the end of the season. You understand, I know her no better than I knew the old lady."

"I'm still not quite sure what relation the present owner is to old Miss Abercrombie."

The curé waved his large, hard-working hands. "She was married to a cousin of the old lady—she herself is a Frenchwoman, now a widow. This house would have come to her husband; I understand there is no son."

"Did she know old Miss A.?" It was very peaceful sitting there in the sun talking to the curé; she felt no hurry to discover the whereabouts of the villa.

"Madame Abercrombie never came in the old lady's lifetime. But the lawyer dealing with the estate put an advertisement in the paper, and Madame saw it and replied."

"Quite a plum to drop into her lap," Sarah commented. "What would have happened if she hadn't turned up?"

"If no legal heir had been found at the end of three months, then the property would have gone to the Ribauds—Martin and Marie. They have been here for twenty years looking after the old lady, and now they serve the new owner."

"It's a bit rough on them," exclaimed Sarah, "this Mrs. Abercrombie suddenly appearing out of the blue. Did they know about the will?"

"People like the Ribauds, mademoiselle, always know."

"They must have been counting on inheriting—unless, of course, they didn't want it."

"In this country all men desire property," the curé told her gravely. "It gives a sense of security to know that the land on which you plant your feet each morning belongs to you; it is like a small taste of eternity. And then, when this elegant lady arrived from Paris . . ." He made Paris sound as remote as a Hottentot settlement.

"It's enough to make the old lady come back and haunt the place," Sarah said lightly. "Oh dear, what have I said? You don't really believe in ghosts?" (All the same, it was odd how much more plausible they seemed here than in Regent's Park, where she and Pat and Polly had their London flat.)

"If there are such creatures they deserve only our compassion," said the old man gently. "After all, mademoiselle, death is only another part of the mystery of life. There was talk enough while the old lady was still with us: that she was a miser, she was a witch, she had a fortune hidden under the floor, she communed with spirits and could foresee the future. All I knew was that she was a lonely woman and, for all her religious fervor, an unhappy one."

"I thought you said she didn't have any religion."

"I said she was not of our faith. But religion, what is that but a way of belief? She belonged to a—movement?" he looked at her questioningly as if he were unsure about the word. "They call themselves the Exclusive Saints, their rules beyond charity. On their account she had to remain alone in the house, since only members of her faith might sleep under the same roof, or eat at her table. Here we have few saints and by their very nature these are not exclusive, since it is of the essence of sainthood to serve."

"But Martin—Marie—what about them?"

(15)

Sarah felt her head start to swim, partly because of this strange old man's peculiar recital, partly perhaps from sitting so long in the burning sun.

"When you are in the villa you will see a little lodge—a cottage—on the grounds, connected with the villa by a telephone. I fear you will find no one there now, since Madame left for her holiday at Biarritz this morning and Martin drove her into Pau to catch her train there. Marie's daughter, Celline, whose husband is a pastry cook at Lourdes, is expecting a child, and Marie has gone to be with her. They did not expect you today, mademoiselle."

"Well no," acknowledged Sarah. "I'm what you might call the advance guard. I'll be able to spy out the land before the others arrive."

"And Madame did not know . . . ?"

"I sent her a telegram, it should have arrived yesterday. Fortunately, she sent us a key when we signed the lease, just in case we should arrive when no one was at home. It won't make any difference, Martin and Marie not being here. I wouldn't have let them stay anyhow; I expect they need their holiday."

"You mean you are prepared to stay alone in the house?"

"Old Miss Abercrombie was alone, wasn't she—at night anyhow. And in a solitary place like this we're not likely to be troubled with prowlers. The only person who could disturb me would be the ghost, and you've just assured me I would have no reason to be afraid of her. It sounds an awful life," she added, with a little shiver, despite the heat of the sun. "I don't suppose there were any other Exclusive Saints around. I suppose you don't know whether the new owner has ever had any—manifestations? Or perhaps she's not the nervous type."

"Mrs. Abercrombie is never alone there," the curé told her.

"Visitors?"

"Not so far as I know, mademoiselle, but one or other of the Ribauds is always with her."

"You mean they keep her prisoner?"

"I understand it is at her own wish. It is a lonely house, she is accustomed to cities. And there are strange tales told."

"You mean tramps breaking in for buried treasure or something? Surely she can't believe that."

"Human nature is very fallible, mademoiselle. And places have their own atmosphere, carry their own message. But even in old Miss Abercrombie's day the house was never left unoccupied. I would see her sometimes in the old black motor, with Martin at the wheel, and the old one wrapped in a brown fur ulster. She wore it all the year round. It was as rough as a bear. Yes, that was how she looked. She was not a large woman, you understand—a shrewmouse wrapped in a bear's pelt."

"Sounds fascinating," Sarah murmured. "And Marie kept the ghost company? Anyway, it's only for a few days."

The curé pulled a huge old silver watch out of his pocket. "You must forgive me, mademoiselle, I am delaying you. I am a garrulous old man, but a new face here is a gift from heaven. If I can be of service everyone knows where I may be found."

"It was the villa really," Sarah recalled. "I mean, I can't find it."

The curé smiled, pointing down the lane.

"But there's only a sort of canal there."

"A water-splash, swelled perhaps by the recent rains. Simply drive on. Your car will suffer no more than a little mud."

"How on earth do pedestrians get through? Or are they expected to bring their bathing suits?"

He looked puzzled and she stepped up and down the road, drawing her skirt tight, moving delicately, like someone trying to wade through an incoming tide.

The curé's laugh was as hearty as the cawing of a flight of rooks.

"Bravo, mademoiselle. If you had looked you would see a bridge—a log in fact—set at the side, to prevent wet feet. But so few people go that way. The villa has never had visitors.

(17)

There is only Armande. He brings the ice for the icebox, any letters there may be. He would think nothing of a little water. Oh, the Council was prepared to mend the road if Miss Abercrombie would contribute to the cost, but she said that when providence had offered her a natural barrier against the world, the flesh and the devil, she would be mad to pay to have it removed."

"She sounds as nutty as a fruitcake," acknowledged Sarah candidly. "Still, if she hasn't haunted Mrs. Abercrombie, why should she haunt me? Well, I'll brave the incoming tide, and I shall remember your offer," she added. "Perhaps I ought to tell you that, like her, I don't belong to your church."

"I am the shepherd of all the sheep," said the curé simply. "Now when you are through the lake," his eyes twinkled, "you must look out for a signpost with the name of the house. Up a short lane and you will find the gates."

He watched her get into the little red car and drive away; she bumped over the stones and ruts and was through the water-splash almost before she realized it. Still the house remained invisible and she almost overshot the signpost before she recognised it. Then out of the tail of her eye she saw it, and backing carefully, turned into the lane. It was a relief to find that the big iron gates enclosing the villa opened at her touch. Once she had closed them behind her she felt as shut off from the familiar world as if she had walked through the gate of death. The silence seemed complete. Not even a bird cheeped or rustled among the leaves; the cicadas—or bees—had finished their meeting and gone home. The wind that had cooled the golden air during the earlier part of the day had dropped completely and heat, like a blanket, covered the world.

"Remote, restful and romantic"—that was how the advertisement had described the house. Remote it certainly was, but romantic! She controlled a shudder. It had a blank idiot's face, a big flat door painted black, two oblong windows like pendulous cheeks and two small crooked windows—attics those would be—for eyes. The grass in front was badly tended; presumably the strawberry and asparagus beds of which Mrs. Abercrombie had written so lyrically were at the back.

I see the curé's point of view, she assured herself. It wasn't surprising either that Mrs. Abercrombie, that elegant Parisian, didn't care to remain here alone.

She swerved to the left toward what was presumably the garage, and stopped dead. Because the curé was wrong about one thing anyway. The villa wasn't deserted; the garage was blocked by a biggish old-fashioned black car.

2

Someone must have heard her drive up, because as she alighted the front door opened and a man appeared. He was very good-looking in a dark Southern fashion, with brilliant almost black eyes under black brows. He seemed rather informally dressed, and his manner was easy—jaunty almost. But his eyes were wary.

Charming! Sarah thought. I needn't have gone further than The Whipsnade zoo if all I'd wanted was a wolf for companion.

"Miss Hollis?" he said, coming to meet her. "This is a surprise."

He spoke English quite well; perhaps Miss Abercrombie's religion hadn't allowed her to use the French language, and twenty years is a long time.

"I sent a telegram," Sarah explained. "Don't tell me it didn't arrive."

"Oh yes, it has arrived. But it said the day after tomorrow, so we supposed . . ."

"We? Oh, of course—Marie, your wife."

"She has gone to stay with her daughter."

Before he could say any more a woman's voice called from the villa, "Who is it, Martin?" and someone else appeared on the scene. Mrs. Abercrombie presumably, Sarah decided. Even without Martin's assurance, she would never have mistaken this woman for Marie Ribaud. She was a little on the plump side for English views on beauty, but she had a fine bosom and beautiful legs tapering to shapely feet. Her brown eyes were full of vitality, and she, too, spoke English, though with a stilted accent so that no one could have mistaken her nationality. A Frenchwoman married to an Englishman, Sarah recalled.

"Mrs. Abercrombie?" she said quickly. "I'm afraid there's been a muddle, but it really wasn't my fault. The telegram must have got delayed. I certainly meant to tell you I would be coming today."

"I'm just driving Madame into Pau," said Martin in a casual, slightly impudent voice. "Later I could come back and show Miss Hollis over her property." His dark eyes smiled insolently into hers. "There is no time to go over the house now," he added in authoritative tones. "I will bring round the car. Mademoiselle will understand . . ."

"You don't have to bother to come back," said Sarah quickly. "I'm sure I shall find my way about all right. If there's anything I don't understand I could telephone you at Lourdes, couldn't I?"

Surprise for an instant held him dumb. Then "Lourdes, Miss Hollis?"

"I met the curé at the top of the road. He told me Marie would be there—I suppose until we were expected—and I gathered you would be with her. I don't want to upset anyone's plans, and I don't suppose," she added, aware of an oddness about the silence of the other two, "I shall have to bother you at all."

"So you met the curé," said Martin.

"He showed me how to get here. Nobody mentioned the

water-splash. He was quite informative about old Miss Abercrombie, too; told me not to be afraid of ghosts—not that I believe in them, of course, but if I did, this is the sort of place where I'd expect to find them."

"There are no ghosts here," said Martin. "Old Miss Abercrombie would never have allowed it. Oh, people talked, there's so little to talk about here. Madame's left one room locked with all her things in it . . ." He seemed to have taken complete charge of the situation.

Sarah found herself wondering how Marie viewed this new household where Martin so clearly held sway. She said quickly, to the woman, "I mustn't hold you up. It would be dreadful if you missed your train—Biarritz, isn't it? I'm very glad to have met you though—the curé seemed to think I was too late—and if we should get into any sort of muddle I can always telephone."

"But there is no telephone at Lourdes," Martin said. "Madame has left a note about the hot-water heater. The wells should be full with the weather we have had, and there is an extra rain tub in the garden—the water is very soft. The electric plant is in a building outside, the house makes its own electricity. In addition, there are lamps—you can get oil from the garage where you get gas for your car. I shall be back later to explain . . ."

She was standing by this time in a big bleak hall, and she remembered Crook's joke about the House of Usher. It seemed less of a joke at close quarters. Steep stairs rose to a dark landing. There seemed an unusual number of doors; no doubt some of them belonged to cellars or cupboards. She wished she had arrived earlier in the day. Martin departed rather abruptly to fetch the car; presumably the luggage had been loaded on already.

Sarah reverted to the problem of the telegram. "I don't understand how it could have got delayed."

"It would be on account of Armande," said the cool voice of the woman beside her. "He is not quite—you understand—but in a village one uses what is at hand. He was given the telegram no doubt; he forgot to bring it. It is he who brings the milk from the farm," she added. "He brought it this morning—probably afraid of telegrams. The villagers think they bring bad luck."

"There is one thing," said Sarah. "The money for the extra week's rent. We paid the rest into your account as you asked, but—I could settle it in cash if you like. I brought the currency—Pat's going to bring the traveler's checks."

"Pat?" The dark, thick brows lifted. "You did not speak . . ."

"I said there were three of us girls—I'm sure I mentioned all our names. Not that it matters. Pat's really the business head."

The woman's face cleared. "Yes. Of course. Now remember, Martin will tell you anything you wish. Do not allow anything the curé said to trouble you. He is a talky old man, though the peasants round here like him well enough. It is a pity you had to come by yourself . . ."

"I shan't mind," Sarah assured her. "I really wanted a few days alone. . . . What did Miss Abercrombie die of?"

She asked the question idly and was surprised by the pause that followed it.

"I never saw her; she was an old woman." The voice made no attempt to conceal indifference. "She lived as she wished. . . . You spoke of the rent, mademoiselle?"

"Yes, of course." Sarah produced a wallet and counted out some bills. There were whisked into Madame's bag as the door opened and Martin reappeared. He looked from one woman to the other in rather a startled way.

"I am ready, Martin," said Madame. "You will be all right here," she added to Sarah. "It seems a large house at first, but you need not use all of it, and when your friends come and Martin and Marie are back . . ."

"You mustn't worry about me," said Sarah firmly. "I'm accustomed to looking after myself, and there'll be people in the village. I mean, I have to buy food and there's a garage, I suppose . . ."

"Monsieur Binet," said Martin. "I hear he still has that

young Englishman working for him while his own son is in military service."

"I told you I should soon make friends," promised Sarah, cheering up again. "That's two already."

"The curé is a very busy man . . ."

"I wasn't thinking of the curé." She'd remembered the card Crook had insisted on her taking. She wouldn't need it, of course, but it was like having an emergency five-pound note in your pocket. It suggested security. "You mustn't miss your train on my account," she said.

She wondered, after they had gone, about the relationship between them. She wouldn't trust Martin any farther than she could throw him. He might look bland enough on the surface, but most likely in his heart he hated the woman who had appeared from nowhere and deprived him of his inheritance. I wonder if she's doing anything for them by way of compensation, she reflected, fetching her case from the trunk of the little red car. You'd think she'd feel some responsibility. The point was, would Madame's ideas of what was right approximate his? He's playing her like a fish, she told herself, climbing stairs so steep she couldn't imagine how an old woman had ever crawled up and down them. The funny thing is she looks hooked, too. Of course, he is a handsome beast and she's a widow—only what's Marie going to say?

She had an uncomfortable feeling that she might have stepped into a plot unawares. If Martin wanted something, you could be pretty sure he'd get it; he wanted the villa, and by hook or crook she had a feeling he might get that, too. A bit of luck for Madame, really, that she had these friends in Biarritz. Being poor and alone may not be much fun but being rich—or comparatively rich—and solitary can spell danger with a capital D. She found herself wishing Martin wasn't coming back tonight. Not that he could do her any harm, of course, but she'd like the house better when Marie was there, too, to say nothing of Pat and Polly.

The house had to be seen to be believed. Some doors she opened and shut at once; the rooms seemed great cold barns stored with old furniture, old trunks, piles of books mildewed with damp. There was an enormous kitchen with a rusty range and pans big enough to cook a baby in; it was a relief to find there was also a modern one with an electric stove and water heater.

When she got upstairs and started looking in the bedrooms she forgot her apprehensions, which vanished like cobwebs before the broom. Unparalleled views, the advertisement had said, and in this respect at least it had not lied. Now in the golden light of late afternoon the mountains stood brilliant, crowned with snow against a magical sky. In the garden under the window of the room she picked for herself, rose bushes glowed in circular beds. Somewhere out of sight would be the strawberry and asparagus beds, the lettuces and herbs. Some birds were singing, invisible in the blue—I never knew birds sang at night, she thought—and on the skyline she saw the outline of a church with a tall, narrow steeple. Presumably another village. When Martin came back she would find out if there was a road, and also inquire about getting food supplies. It didn't seem likely there'd be many deliveries in this remote place.

She still didn't like the look of him, or his proprietorial air toward the woman who presumably paid his wages. She began to wonder about old Miss Abercrombie who had died. Had she perhaps been completely under the Ribauds' thumbs? Anything could have happened here, and who would know? The answer to that was that somehow the curé would have found out. Still, even he didn't know everything. He knew about Martin taking Madame to Pau this morning, but he didn't know about her stealing back again after Marie had gone. It was no wonder they had both looked so taken aback, so guilty. What was the secret? Lovers, she wondered? But surely not here, under Marie's eye. A more sinister thought occurred to her. Martin, a go-getter if ever she had seen one, might be making up to the widow for his own ends. In which case Marie was presumably in the plot.

"I wish he wasn't coming back," she said aloud. "But perhaps she's afraid I shall blow up the villa." It wouldn't be surprising, seeing the antediluvian nature of the hot-water system. Then she rebuked herself. The sun's gone to your head, or perhaps it's the local atmosphere. No doubt there is a perfectly simple explanation why Mrs. Abercrombie returned. It was so simple she failed to see what it was.

She was having a makeshift supper from the supplies she had brought with her when the telephone rang, and she hastened to answer it. Someone who didn't know Madame was gone—or possibly the good curé telephoning to make sure she had got in safely. To her surprise it was Martin's voice at the other end of the line.

"There has been an accident, mademoiselle," he said, and her heart jumped like a frog. She hadn't thought to ask the curé what would happen to the property if Mrs. Abercrombie died.

"To Mrs. Abercrombie?" she said.

"No, no." He laughed easily. "Why should you think that, Miss Hollis? Some fool left a nail in the middle of the road, the car ran over it, we had a puncture. By the time I had changed the tire and driven Madame to the station the train had gone. Since Madame is meeting her friends at Biarritz tomorrow I shall be driving her in."

"All that way?" she exclaimed, and he said, "Even if there were a plane, Madame does not care to fly, and there is no other train tonight." He had rung up to explain that he wouldn't be returning, after all. It's an ill wind that blows no one any good, Sarah recalled. It was the sort of cliché Arthur Crook loved.

"There's really no necessity for you to come back at all before next week," she told Martin. "I'm finding my way round and if I do get into any difficulties I shan't hesitate to ask the curé's advice."

He hesitated. "If Madame agrees . . ."

"Why shouldn't she agree? Does she think I shall try and probe the secret of the locked room?"

Her rather feeble joke fell quite flat. "Pardon, mademoiselle," murmured the man.

"You can assure her I'm house-trained; I shan't set the place on fire. I mean to be out most of the time anyway; this weather's too gorgeous for hanging about a house. So please tell her not to worry."

"I will tell her what you say, mademoiselle," returned Martin sedately. "You will be sure to lock the door at nights? Sometimes vagrants try to get in, thinking perhaps the villa is unoccupied."

"I won't forget," she promised.

It was still too early to think of bed after she had rung off, so she decided to start a letter to the girls at home.

"Don't leave out a single detail," they had said. Well, she had plenty to tell them.

"I can't hope to do justice to this house," she began. "It has to be seen to be believed. Mrs. A. says it harbors no ghosts, and so does the curé, but you don't have to believe them. If you should open your eyes to find a mysterious figure standing beside your bed, don't say you weren't warned."

Close at hand someone screamed and she dropped her pen. But it was only a jet plane splitting the skies with a noise like rending silk.

"I can't imagine how we ever complained of the lions roaring in the zoo," she went on. "You won't find anything as friendly as a lion here. Martin is definitely a wolf."

Her pen flew over the paper; she told them about Crook and the curé and just writing about those two imperturbable men calmed her spirits.

"The mountains are everything Mrs. A. claims for them. Tomorrow I shall go out and explore . . ."

Suddenly the storm burst; the sky was now almost black; down came the rain like a pack of demoniac horses jostling through the dark; and after the thunder came the lightning in long silver gashes. The house was too strongly built to shake, but everything in it responded to the storm. Strong hands rattled the windows, thudded at the doors. The curtains on their old-fashioned wooden rings came sliding along their polished rails. Shrieks came through the keyholes, but of course that was only the wind. She put down her pen and looked out at the unpopulated world; there wasn't a light to be seen anywhere; she could just make out a black hump that was the Ribauds' cottage. Poor Martin, she thought, driving into Biarritz in this. Only perhaps he wasn't. Perhaps the story of the accident was just an excuse, so that he needn't come back tonight. Perhaps the pair of them were laughing together over the subterfuge at this very instant.

The storm came sailing like a bomb across the valley; it clattered from the distant mountains and wept like a giant Niobe against the villa wall. The faint light of the bulb filled the room with shadows; the walls seemed to be whispering. How could I have complained of the noise at Alicante? she thought. It was heaven, heaven, all that life. That was what Crook had meant, of course. "It's a pity he's not here," she said aloud. She'd be sorry for any ghost that tried to stalk him. It would be only too glad to get back to its nice, safe grave and pull its shroud over its dessicated bones, and swear to abandon haunting for the rest of eternity.

She braved the stairs presently—the rest of the letter must wait till morning—found a box of candles and recklessly lighted half a dozen, sticking them all around her room, and to hell with wax on the furniture. The little flames were oddly reassuring, as they bowed and curtsied in the wind but refused to be extinguished. She fell asleep suddenly with them watching around her, like the childish angels on Christmas cards when she herself had been a child. And presently the rain ceased, the wind dropped, the Valkyrie retreated and the valley slept. And Sarah slept with it.

3

Morning dawned in a glory of blue and gold. In the garden the roses tossed, undefeated; against the skyline the mountains waited, across the valley was a village of houses that might have come out of a child's picture book. They were white houses with straight lines, neat rows of windows, pointed roofs of pale gray or pale blue slate. A little church with a pointed belfry tower dominated them; trees, tall and dark as sentinels, held their own against the radiant peaks. Sarah stood, letting the peace and the power of the scene sweep over her. Last night was like a bad dream now; even Martin and Mrs. Abercrombie were no more than shadows. Presently she hunted out the binoculars she had brought to identify birds; she saw none that appeared familiar, but she did discern a lake, dark and deep as a tarn, green against the prevailing cool walls of the houses—the sort of lake, cool and deep, where heathen rites to Artemis might have been celebrated.

She found her way to the bathroom and experimented with

the hot-water heater. The little light came on, she waited, and the water ran. It was soft and faintly brown, like peat water. She cooked herself a huge breakfast from her supplies, decided to unpack, get the geography of the house by heart, and then drive out to that celestial view. It should be possible to bathe in that lake. A whole week, she thought, a week of exquisite solitude, a week in which she could recover her balance and realize that there is an end even to the end of the world.

Driving out of the big iron gates she took a right turn to avoid the water-splash, but the road petered out into pasture. There was nothing to do but reverse the car and go back the way she had taken the previous afternoon. The villa this morning looked more like a fortress than the monastery it had once been, protected on one side by the water-splash and on the other by overgrown fields. Of course, that sort of protection cut both ways. If it was difficult for enemies to get in, it was equally difficult for the besieged to get out. She raced through the splash and up the hill to the high road; this was the main road of the district, but everything moved so slowly here, it was like regressing through time to a quieter if no less sinister age. There was little traffic and no people. Later, she decided—anyway before the others arrived—she must explore marketing possibilities, arrange about milk and bread, but today was hers, a shining gift like a birthday present. She had enough provender for some days yet; this morning she hadn't a care in the world.

It was farther to the mountains than had appeared from the window—all of thirty-five miles—but motoring was a joy in such conditions. The little town when she reached it was as fairylike as it had seemed from the window. She ran the car through the toylike main street and saw the lake, glittering darkly, far beneath. An enterprising company had put up a restaurant with a balcony overlooking the water with its dense fringe of trees. She left the car on the road and began to descend by a flight of steps. The first flight led to a second, and now the silence was broken by the wailing of a child.

The restaurant itself came into view, a long cool roof, and some tables on a balcony overlooking the lake. There were no customers and none seemed expected.

A motherly-looking woman in white was walking up and down with a dark-eyed baby in her arms; a very young man, hardly more than a boy, sat on the edge of one of the tables, laughing. When he saw a customer he sprang up, seeming dumfounded with astonishment. But he quickly recovered, pulled out a chair from one of the tables, and soon Sarah was lunching on freshly made *canelloni* and delicious white grapes. The wine she ordered was pale gold; the coffee that followed, black and hot. She sat drowsing in the sun for a little, before she started on her descent to the lake for the first swim of the holiday. The deep green water looked very cold. She changed among some trees and dived in. After the first shock she became accustomed to the temperature and swam about like a young seal. No one approached her; she might have been alone in the world. If a spirit had come from among the trees or risen from the depths of the lake, she would scarcely have been surprised.

Coming presently from that world of shadows into the brilliant sunlight, she found the hotel closed and still, not a human creature to be seen. A metal blind had been drawn over the front of the restaurant; the chairs on the balcony were tilted against the bare tables; even the vivid blue birds in a cage on the wall slept with their heads beneath their wings.

On the upper road the little red car baked in the sun, since there was no shade available, and the leather seats were hot to the touch. The whole village slept, blinds were drawn in the houses, shops closed. London—Simon—the world of fashion magazines in which she worked for forty-eight weeks of the year—seemed as remote as the moon. She started the motor and set out on the return journey.

It happened so suddenly she couldn't have named the precise instant when the little car went out of control. Braking as she rounded a corner and crossed a little bridge, she realized she was getting no response. Hand brake and foot brake alike seemed to have ceased to function. The road here ran steeply downhill; her speed increased; she ran over a stone and almost turned turtle. At the foot of the hill she must turn a blind corner with who knew what coming toward the curve. A long olive-green Panther came purring by, missing her by inches, as she fought with the wheel to keep the car steady. Down it went and out of sight.

He must have seen me, thought Sarah. Why didn't he stop and offer to help? Afraid I might crash him perhaps.

The power that is said to look out for fools and children finally intervened in the form of a small rise in the level of the road, which enabled her to pull up shakily on a patch of grass just before the curve. The sudden jolt with which the car came to a halt didn't do it any good, but at least she was alive. As she opened the door and staggered out, she felt the whole world turning topsy-turvy. Viewing the car, now set down as bland as a cat, it was impossible to realize what it had put her through during the past—how long? Two minutes? Three? In crises like these one lost all sense of time, she didn't realize how long she had been waiting when another car came by—a black one this time, but it didn't stop either. There was a long pause and then a truck appeared. The driver winked and gave her the V-sign, but he didn't pull up. Girls sitting on the grass beside immobilized cars seemed part of the day's work to him. She looked up and down the road as if she expected to see a yellow auto-club box and find herself in an English country lane, but there was nothing. The light was like a curtain of gold, so heavy that a passing bee seemed to be supported by it rather than by its own wings. Overhead some birds went by, too far off for identification, and unless they were members of a pigeon post patrol they wouldn't have been any use anyway. She did think of looking under the hood of the car but abandoned that notion; she was no mechanic. This is where I need Martin, she reflected wryly. The irony of the notion made her laugh; she must have still been laughing when, exhausted by heat, fear and subsequent relief, she fell asleep.

She woke suddenly with a sense of being watched, and opened her eyes to see a young man standing beside a motorcycle, his helmet over his arm, his goggles pushed up over sharp gray eyes.

"In trouble?" he inquired sympathetically.

"I was asleep," announced Sarah.

"That's what I thought. You must have been having a pleasant dream. You were laughing."

"Was I? I can't think why. My car's come to grief; nobody would stop. I thought if someone would take a message to the nearest garage . . ."

"There isn't one for miles," he told her cheerfully. "And that's shut today."

She was inclined to be indignant. "What happens to cars that get into trouble?"

"That's their problem, isn't it? What happened?"

"You tell me. And don't suggest I've run out of gas, because I haven't."

"It has been known to happen," he reminded her. He peeled off his thick driving gloves. "Mind if I take a look?"

"That's what I hoped."

He lifted the hood. "Marvelous what these little Arkwrights will do. Look as if they're made of a couple of cracker tins . . . Got a wrench?"

"Yes." She began to laugh again.

"You *are* easy to amuse, aren't you? Did I say something funny?"

"I was just thinking. The last film I went to there was a girl whose car broke down and a stranger came along and asked for a wrench and then—then he hit her on the head with it."

"Oh, I'd bring my own wrench for that," he assured her. "It 'ud be heavier. Besides, there must have been a reason, or did he make a hobby of hitting blondes over the head?"

He had his own head inside the hood as he spoke. "You been tinkering with this?" he inquired.

(33)

"I told you . . ."

"Well then, got any enemies? If not, you've been pretty unlucky."

"I don't know what you mean. I've only just arrived."

"I noticed this was an English registration."

"And if I do have enemies they aren't on this side of the Channel. Besides, the car was running all right this morning. What's wrong?"

"A nut's worked loose. I don't say it couldn't have happened on its own, only it very seldom does. It's a miracle really you didn't turn over."

His face was very stern. "You don't really think I did it myself?" exclaimed Sarah incredulously.

"It hadn't occurred to me, I must admit. I mean, if you wanted to commit suicide, there are lots of less painful ways —less messy, too. There's a pond not far away . . ."

"If you mean the lake . . ."

"It looks like a pond to me. Well, you'll be all right now, but it wouldn't do any harm giving your car a general overhaul if you're planning to do much driving on these roads. They were meant for soldiers or horses, not for a delicate job like a motorcar."

"I'm very grateful," said Sarah, producing her pack of cigarettes and offering it. "I began to wonder if I should spend the night here."

"I've spent it in worse places."

"Two cars did pass, but they wouldn't stop."

"Probably thought you were the original Lorelei. Your pond—sorry, lake—would come in very useful."

"Who are you?" asked Sarah curiously.

"I hoped you'd get around to that. John Bryce is the name, and"—he started to feel in his pocket—"if you should feel like giving the car the once-over, here's the place to come. I'll promise it personal attention."

She looked at the card he gave her. "You're the young Englishman at the garage—the owner's son is in service."

"How talk gets around! Yes, it's true. I'm working there just for the summer, before I take on my first job. I came down from Oxford last year. I've got a work permit, you needn't look prim."

"I didn't know anyone could."

"My mother was French, her brother pulled a string or two. It's what's called a vacational job. You here on a holiday?"

She nodded. "I'm waiting for my friends to join me. They couldn't get away yet."

"Working women? How about you, though? Well, come on. You haven't even given me a name yet, or told me where you're staying."

So she told him. He whistled softly.

"The haunted villa? You've got a nerve. Everyone hereabouts knows the old lady was a miser and comes back at midnight to guard her hoard. Did you say you were alone?"

"Just at the moment. There's a married couple attached to the villa who'll be back next week. Mrs. Abercrombie did ask if I minded, but I said of course not. Anyway, I don't believe in ghosts."

"Wait till you've been at the villa for a week," threatened the young man.

"If old Miss Abercrombie could face it all these years, I can manage for a week. I suppose it's because of her that Martin talks such good English," she added inconsequentially.

"I believe the old lady wouldn't have French spoken—part of her religion perhaps. Anyway, it was her privilege." He shrugged. "France is the land of the free. They don't mind you being a bit eccentric, so long as you're not actually dangerous. By the way, is it true there's a fortune buried in the cellar?"

"That's just local gossip," said Sarah scornfully.

"How can you be so sure when you've only just arrived?"

"The curé told me," Sarah explained. "Apparently Mrs. Abercrombie, the new owner, poohpoohs the idea, too. She was just leaving for her exotic holiday when I drove up last night, the unexpected and, I felt, unwelcome guest."

"Oh come," protested Johnny, "guests don't pay rent, and according to what I hear, that one would charge moths who nested in a blanket. All the same," he frowned, "I don't like the idea of your being there alone."

"Oh nonsense, these aren't the days of Queen Victoria. In any case, it's not for long. Martin and Marie come back next week, and Pat and Polly from England. And it makes a nice change from Regent's Park," she added airily.

"So that's where you live? Close to the Zoological Gardens. You must be quite used to wolves."

"Meaning Martin?"

"So you had noticed? He's the local Casanova all right, got a girl friend tucked away somewhere, an actress or something. One wonders what his wife thinks about it."

"If she knows."

"Don't they always know in France? I thought it was rather expected of you. Still, she must have got his measure long ago. She's older than he is, a widow with a daughter when he surfaced from nowhere near the end of the war. The girl's never lived at home for years, in domestic service before she married, I believe."

"What a lot everyone here knows about everybody else's business! Well, thank you for doctoring my car. Perhaps I shall be able to do as much for you one day."

"That sounds as though you expected us to meet again."

"I'm going to be at the villa for a month, and I shall need gas, if nothing else. Besides, there's that overhaul you spoke of. Anyway, why not look me up at the house of mystery one of these evenings?" she added impetuously.

"I might take you up on that. Just to make sure no ghost's been walking."

Sarah turned the ignition key and heard the engine's familiar throb. "Burning to be off as always," she added. "Don't forget, drop by some time. I really mean it."

She shot off, but a minute or two later he came roaring past her, waved and was gone.

She came back yearning for tea; it was odd how that Victorian gesture stayed with you. But as she climbed out of the car to open the gates she got a fresh shock. The entire space in front of the garage was occupied by an olive-green Panther. She left her little car in the path, and as she came marching up to the house someone called, "Is that you, Cousin Margaret?" and a very tall man with eyes of a remarkably dark blue, strolled around the side of the villa.

"Blow me down!" he said elegantly. "I gathered that you were a lady of—well, mature charms. What a pleasant surprise!"

"Keep your congratulations," Sarah advised him coolly. "I'm simply the present tenant of the villa. Mrs. Abercrombie is in Biarritz. I didn't realize she had any cousins," she added impulsively.

"Possibly she doesn't either, and I don't think it's going to be a rapturous meeting of the clans. Well, a person can hardly be expected to enjoy being told she is occupying a house on false pretenses."

"You'll have to take that up with her when she comes back," suggested Sarah mildly. "Is that your car outside? I suppose it would have killed you to stop and lend me a hand when you passed me on the road this afternoon."

"If you were the one cavorting about in a little red wheelbarrow, yes, most probably it would. What on earth were you doing? Practicing for a circus turn?"

"A nut had mysteriously worked loose," Sarah told him.

"In that case you're probably lucky to be alive. Mechanically minded?"

"No. Someone kindly stopped." She took the key to the villa out of her pocket.

"Do make yourself at home," the young man encouraged her. "I'm sure I couldn't want a nicer tenant."

"You! You haven't told me who you are yet."

(37)

"You didn't ask me. Oliver Abercrombie; the old lady, recently deceased, was my aunt."

"The brother who ran away," exclaimed Sarah. "You're his son."

"You worked that one out very quickly. Do we go in?"

"I can't stop you, can I?"

"I do love your welcoming tone. Are they all like you in the old country?"

"Everyone I have met so far has warned me against unknown men," Sarah told him solemnly. "I don't want to seem inhospitable, but you must realize I've only got your word for it that you're a relative of old Miss A. She doesn't seem to have known anything about you. I mean, you weren't specifically mentioned in the will."

"You don't waste much time, do you? How long did you say you'd been here?"

He followed her into the house and stood staring about him. "Jehoshaphat! Is this the family mansion? No wonder my father couldn't take it. Talk about the cave of—who was it? Sinbad?"

"That one glowed with jewels. You won't find any here."

She went through two huge deserted rooms, followed by Oliver Abercrombie, who looked around with an air of fascinated horror. "Did the old lady live here alone?"

"She had Martin and Marie. They . . ."

"Yes, I've heard about them. No one else?"

"So far as I know, there wasn't anyone else. Anyway, her religion . . ."

"You mean, she stuck to that to the bitter end? My father told me a piece; he didn't tell me the half."

"Is he—I mean . . ."

"You mean, is he dead, my father? Yes. And my mother. And if Aunt Harriet didn't know about me, it's because letters from the unregenerate were returned unopened. My father wrote twice, so he told me. I've no proof naturally, as the first was written at the time of his marriage and the second when I was born. Both letters were returned, unopened, as I said."

"If they didn't know your address . . ."

"In civilized countries it's customary to put your address on the envelope. It was the old man—my grandfather—who sent them back, and I suppose by the time he'd passed on, it was too late for his daughter to try and pick up the threads. You never saw her? The old lady, I mean?"

"She's been dead for some months. I don't imagine that she would have let the villa to strangers. But I suppose it doesn't mean much to Mrs. Abercrombie."

"An easy penny," Oliver agreed. "Where are you going?"

"I was going to put on a kettle, if you've no objections."

"Don't bother," Oliver advised her. "I've got a bottle here."

"Isn't it a bit early for that?" She glanced at the watch on her wrist. "Good heavens, is that the time? I had to hang about for hours before anyone was humane enough to stop on the road and lend me a hand. I've got a bottle of my own," she added, opening a cupboard and taking down some glasses.

"And you're all alone here?"

"Until my friends come over from England next week. An awful lot of people seem to be taking an interest in my welfare," she added.

"I'm sure you must be used to that."

"Let's take our drinks into the other room, shall we?" she asked. "It's more cheerful in there."

"I wouldn't have thought cheerful was quite the word. Go ahead. I'll bring the bottle. You know," he followed at her heels, looking about him at every step, "I didn't know this kind of place existed outside the Victorian novelists." His voice was warm with admiration.

"The whole situation's a bit Victorian, don't you think? The haunted mansion, the missing heir. Tell me more about yourself. When did you realize you were in a position to stake a claim?"

"I hadn't realized I was in the running till I got here. This is actually my first visit to Europe. I'm an American citizen and I've knocked about a lot on the other side of the world;

suddenly I took the notion to come over and see the place where my father lived, though not for very long, when he was a young man. I didn't know my aunt—Miss Abercrombie to you—was dead, though I realized she must be pretty old. She was ten years older than my father, and he wasn't precisely a young man when he married."

"And as soon as you got here you found . . ."

"I heard at St. Crécy, where I'm staying, that she'd died a few months ago. For someone who was practically invisible, people know a lot about her."

"And what they don't know they invent. She's a kind of legend."

Oliver's dark brows lifted. "I thought you hadn't been here long."

"Long enough to have discovered that. Now ask me about the treasure."

"Would you have an answer for me?"

Sarah laughed. "I don't even know that it exists. It's just the sort of place where you'd expect a story like that to spread. But I can tell you one thing: if there ever was a hoard, it won't be there now. I've yet to meet Marie—she's the other half of the married couple, as if you didn't know—but he's the original Geiger counter. If there was gold underground, he'd have found it before now."

"The original Geiger counter and the original computer, what a combination."

"They had the place to themselves for several weeks while the lawyer was trying to trace the next-of-kin," insisted Sarah. "That's when he found Mrs. Abercrombie. It's funny they didn't unearth you."

"Well, not really," said Oliver temperately. "We'd dropped out of Aunt Harriet's world. I understand the old man crossed our name out of the family Bible when my father deserted—that's how he regarded it. I suppose if he'd ever heard his only son was working in a circus . . ."

Sarah began to laugh, not attempting to conceal her disbelief.

"Oh no," she said. "Don't tell me he worked in a circus."

"Me, too. Born and bred," Oliver assured her cheerfully. "It has its points, you know, being born under the Big Top. Teaches a chap to stand on his own feet. Of course, to my respectable relations, he was no better than a hobo, and I was a chip off the old block."

"What made him take up that kind of life?" asked Sarah, and he saw she really wanted to know.

"Have you any notion what it was like, trying to make your way without any special training, in the years after the first war?" he demanded, with more warmth than he had hitherto displayed. "No, of course you haven't. My father took anything that offered—he was a dishwasher, a deck hand. Then he got taken on in the circus; that's where he met my mother. I grew up under canvas, and if it was a choice of canvas and this particular roof, I think I was lucky. Mind you, the old man liked the life. He used to say he had the grave behind him and the grave ahead, and on the short road between them he meant to get as much for his money as he could. Not that my father ever touched much money, but he had everything else, until my mother broke her neck, and he died soon afterward. Then I opted out."

"It must have been dreadful for you—about your mother, I mean." She hesitated. "Did you like it—up till then, that is?"

"I can't have been very keen, or I should have stayed. The real answer is no. My grandfather coming out in me perhaps. There's a thing called reversion to type, you see. You see it in animals. You can have a lion who's a winner from the word go. He sires a litter and there's not one among them who is any use in the business. Not that I haven't bummed around a bit in my time," he added. "Now I'm prepared to settle down as a landowner. What is it? Have I said something amusing?"

"Well, really!" Sarah expostulated. "It's the first time I ever heard of anyone 'bumming around' in a Panther."

"I took that for a gambling debt. But you were saying, if there was a treasure hidden under the floor, the enterprising pair would have found it. Wouldn't they turn it over to the authorities?"

(41)

She said simply, "You haven't met Martin. But the curé and Mrs. Abercrombie swear it never existed."

"Still, there must be an income of some sort, unless the old lady lived on an annuity. Even mausoleums like this one have to be kept up. There are taxes, electricity, food, the wages of her precious couple."

"You'd have to ask the lawyer about that."

"You wouldn't know his name?"

"Isn't that dumb of me? I never thought to ask."

"And you don't know Mrs. Abercrombie's address?"

"Martin will be back next week. He might be able to tell you. He seems very much in Mrs. Abercrombie's confidence."

"And you think that's sinister?"

"I'll tell you this," exclaimed Sarah with sudden animation. "I told you I saw them last night, just for a few minutes, and I got the definite impression that in some way she's under his thumb. I don't mean she looked cowed or anything, but he had a sort of proprietorial air."

"Meaning there's been some monkey business and he knows about it? She must have got her marriage certificate or she wouldn't have been allowed to take over—I hear they're very fussy about that sort of thing in France. What's he like?"

"The Casanova type."

"And is she the sort that might respond?"

Sarah felt a sudden distaste for the subject. "How on earth should I know? Anyway Martin's wife lives on the premises, though they're neither of them here at the moment. They had about a week's leave before the influx of tourists, to visit their daughter who's married to a pastry cook near Lourdes."

"How did you come to hear of the place?"

"Mrs. Abercrombie advertised the villa in the London *Record*, and we took it for a month."

"And Martin and Marie are staying on?"

"Yes."

"That sounds to me as though they hadn't found the treasure. No one in their right senses would stay in this chamber of horrors of his own free will—well, you, of course, but that's different. You're the tourist going for a mystery drive; you know the nice char-à-banc will bring you home safely for dinner—at least, that's what you're anticipating."

"You're freezing my blood," she told him pleasantly.

"I mean it. Now listen—what's your name?"

"Sarah Hollis."

"Listen, Sarah. Why don't you get out while the going's good?"

"Now you'd freeze the blood of any good Frenchman who heard you. I've paid a month's rent in advance."

"Well, wait till your friends arrive, but get into a hotel or something, don't stay here alone."

"You're very concerned for my welfare all of a sudden."

"As the villa's owner, I feel responsible."

"You aren't that yet," she pointed out. "You've got to convince the lawyer . . ."

"Oh, don't quibble." He sounded impatient. "I'm in earnest."

"I can see you are. But why should anything happen to me?" (Only something very nearly had.) "I don't stand in the way of anyone's inheritance."

"I wouldn't be too certain."

"What's that supposed to mean?"

"Suppose someone *is* convinced there's treasure here? Wouldn't this be an ideal opportunity to come and search for it? Don't tell me the news doesn't get round in a small place like this. Mrs. A. is going, Martin and Marie will be out of the way for once—no one stands between X and a possible fortune—I only say possible—except a crazy English girl. Accidents happen very easily. How many people know you're here?"

"Pat and Polly, of course."

"And if they don't hear from you for a few days they won't be alarmed. Who else?"

"The curé."

"Who's probably got his hands full without one feather-brained tourist, probably not even of his persuasion."

"I don't think that fact would bother him. I've got his

address, and he said if I was in any trouble I could contact him."

"If you were in the sort of trouble I envisage, you wouldn't be able to contact him. Does it occur to you that if you were to get in someone's way you could vanish like a puff of smoke, anyway long enough for the conspirators to make their getaway?"

"Even in this house there aren't all those places where you could hide a corpse," she protested.

"I've been taking a look round. There's a nice piece of ground belonging to the estate that would serve their purpose admirably. Overgrown, untamed—I doubt if anyone ever goes there."

"You're taking a lot of trouble to get me out," she said curiously. "I'm wondering why."

"That's a good question. Let's say I don't like to see even a stranger run head-on into a blank wall. Listen, I've got my car here, I can take you anywhere you like, just till your friends arrive."

"Mrs. Abercrombie expects me to be looking after her house."

"She was quite prepared to leave it untenanted for a week."

"She'd probably have padlocks on all the doors if she'd thought it was going to be left empty."

"You look quite an intelligent girl," Oliver continued. "Doesn't it occur to you that a place like this, practically off the map, is a gift to tramps, vagabonds, men hiding from the law—it needn't even be someone who's interested in the mythical treasure. From outside it looks as empty as a new tomb . . ."

"You do think of the most appropriate phrases. What am I expected to do? Run up a flag like the Queen of England to show I'm in residence?"

"I can see I'm wasting my time. By the way, where do Marie and Martin live when they're here?"

"They have a sort of lodge; you must have seen it while you were waiting for me."

"I did wonder. Well, I might doss down there for a few days just till your friends come."

"How do you propose to get in? You can be sure they'll have locked that. And if you were thinking of a window, there's something called breaking and entering. Or do you really think the hidden treasure is under the floor?"

"It wouldn't surprise me particularly. Look, I'm in earnest. Get out."

"What really interests me is why you should be so concerned for my safety."

"I suppose you'd die laughing if I said my chief concern was that nothing should happen to you—on my premises."

"Why should you worry? Just one more ghost . . ."

"I should like to shake you till your teeth rattled," he said. "Though in point of fact, my sympathy should be reserved for any interloper crazy enough to break in. Still, if you should wake up one morning and find you've been eliminated overnight, remember you were warned. You won't mind my running in to make sure all's well, I suppose?"

"Visitors always welcome. You know, before I came here, Pat—that's one of the three of us girls—said, 'I do hope you won't be bored until we arrive.' That's about the last thing I'm likely to be. Always something happening at Little Puddlecombe."

"I'm afraid I don't know it," said Oliver politely.

"Oh, that's just an old village saying."

"Really? I suppose you wouldn't be open to giving me lessons in colloquial English?"

"You are a trier, aren't you? But, for one thing, I'm not a schoolmistress, and for another, I'm here on holiday."

"I was afraid you might say that. Next time we meet we must sample my bottle. I'm afraid we've made that one of yours look a bit silly. You know," he added casually, as they threaded their way back to the front door, "it's a pity you aren't a member of the family. I feel my aunt would have approved of you as an heir."

4

After Oliver had departed, returning to his hotel at St. Crécy, the village beyond St. Mariole, Sarah made herself an omelette and opened a jar of Stilton. Tomorrow I must go to market, she decided. Well, it's been quite a day. If anything else happens I shall probably collapse like a Victorian heroine.

She was washing up in the kitchen when the telephone rang. The curé? she thought, perplexed. Oliver? Johnny? But it wasn't any of them. She couldn't mistake the voice on the other end of the line.

"Mrs. Abercrombie! But I thought—I mean, I didn't know they had telephones on yachts."

"I am not yet on the yacht. Miss Hollis, I am troubled about you being alone in that house. If I had known . . ."

"It's becoming monotonous," said Sarah, "the number of people who want me to get out."

"Who else?" The voice sharpened.

"Well—Oliver, for one."

"Oliver?"

"Oliver Abercrombie. He says—I hope this won't come as too much of a shock—he says the late Miss Abercrombie was his aunt, and that that makes him next-of-kin."

There was a long moment of silence. Then "This person who claims to be Oliver Abercrombie—where did he come from?"

"America, I think. He said he hadn't known Miss Abercrombie was dead till he arrived in the neighborhood, but since he was over here he thought he'd look up the old homestead. I suppose they told him the address in the village—he seemed surprised to find me there."

"And he told you he was Oliver Abercrombie?"

"Yes. He wanted your address but of course I couldn't give it to him. Then he wanted to know the lawyer's address. Then he wanted me to clear out. He said it wasn't safe . . ."

"Not safe?"

"Well—tramps, treasure-seekers, you know."

"Miss Hollis, I must beg—you will not be flippant."

"Was I?" She was genuinely surprised, more surprised still to find out how cheerful she felt. The result of a few human contacts, presumably, when all you'd expected had been the flap of the crow in the arras, the whisper of dust in the corridors. "I didn't mean it. He's gone, if that's what you're worried about. Now you've telephoned, you could give me the lawyer's address, and next time Oliver Abercrombie comes in . . ."

"He is coming again?"

"He said he might look in to make sure I hadn't joined the galaxy of ghosts. I'm sorry, that was a joke," she wound up hurriedly. "Well, he's not likely to establish a claim before you get back. You know what lawyers are."

"I do not think it will be necessary for me to give you the lawyer's address, Miss Hollis; I do not think this man will trouble Monsieur Dubois. You see, whoever he may be, he cannot be Oliver Abercrombie, because that unfortunate young man was killed in a car crash more than two years ago."

The silence following this statement lasted so long that the words—"Miss Hollis, are you there? Are you still listening?" had been repeated twice before Sarah said vaguely, "Yes, of course. Are you sure?"

"About young Abercrombie? Monsieur Dubois has proof; there was an inquest, a funeral. This man is an impostor."

"Whoever he is he must have known the real Oliver," Sarah urged. "He knew—knows—about the house and the odd religious backgrounds. He said his father—Oliver's father, I mean—worked in a circus."

A snort came over the line. "Is it likely?"

"Is it likely he'd say it if it wasn't true, a fact that could be so easily disproved? Because this lawyer must have made fairly intensive inquiries. And how did he know about the house?"

"Did he tell you any particular detail, Miss Hollis? Or was it general?"

Sarah considered. "He'd heard the story about the buried treasure," she burst out.

The woman laughed scornfully. "He would hear all that at St. Mariole. Even during the old woman's lifetime the legends were rife. Did he have any special knowledge of the house?"

"He seemed appalled by it, said he wasn't surprised his father had wanted to get out. Or words to that effect. His father's dead, did you know?"

"If his father were not dead, then *he* would have inherited. Now, Miss Hollis, try to remember. Did he say anything about this aunt, whose nephew he claims to be, that he could not have learned in a bar in St. Mariole or from a conversation in the Market?"

"I don't know what you can learn in bars and markets," acknowledged Sarah rather tartly. "He spoke of her as Aunt Harriet. Is that her name?"

"That he could easily learn in the village. Did he tell you where he is staying?"

"At St. Crécy—I don't know the name of the hotel, but I daresay there aren't many. I don't think he could have known about you," she added; "he seemed so surprised. And—this'll make you laugh—he actually thought I was the new owner." Even over the telephone line Sarah realized nobody was laughing, not even herself. Mrs. Abercrombie was certainly not amused.

"He arrives at a time when it is known I shall be away, when Martin and Marie are also absent. You say he was surprised to see you? Probably he expected to find the house empty?"

"But why?" clamored Sarah. "What was the point of crossing the world to look at an empty house? Unless, of course, he believes in the legend of the treasure, and thought he'd have a session on his own." She was surprised at her own perspicacity.

"You found him on the doorstep when you returned?"

"Not on the doorstep; he was wandering round the garden. He called me cousin. Actually, I'd seen him before when I had trouble with my car. He went by in a big olive-green Panther he drives. Of course, he didn't know then I was staying here."

"Did he show you photographs—any proofs of identity? You must understand that any impostor could have learned the little he told you. Did you not think that an honest man would have written and waited to know if he were welcome?"

"He wasn't asking to be put up, he came to call," Sarah explained, wondering why on earth she was trying to defend him. "And I suppose he might have tried to telephone, but I've been out all day."

"I do not like it." The voice came firm and assured. "This man is clearly an impostor. Why he is there I do not know, but I cannot have a young English girl there alone."

"I've paid a month's rent," pointed out Sarah mutinously, "and I'm not complaining."

"Nor are you thinking of me. If anything should happen, on my premises, to a young English girl I left there alone, I should feel responsible. There is an inn at St. Mariole—Le Chat Qui Rit. It is not very grand, but you will be in no danger there. Remain for a few days until your friends join you, until Martin and Marie return . . ."

"I'd never hold my head up again," returned Sarah simply, "if I ran away from a house because of a possible ghost and a claimant. Because that's what he is. He thinks by rights it's his property. Perhaps that's why he was so anxious for me to go. The funny thing is he gives precisely the same reason as you do, that I'm not safe here, but I don't see why I should let myself be chased out by him. In an emergency, I could always get in touch with the police."

An angry laugh greeted her words. "The police at St. Mariole, mademoiselle, is one fat old man, awaiting his pension."

"Don't they ever have any crime there?" Sarah demanded.

"They send into St. Crécy where there is a large station. Very well, Miss Hollis, since you will not take my advice and leave the villa, I shall instruct Martin to come back and see that you are not molested."

"Half a minute," said Sarah shrewdly. "Were you expecting something like this? I mean, has anyone else been molested, as you call it?"

"I don't understand you, mademoiselle."

"Has anyone been attacked on the grounds of the villa? Is there something I should know? Everything seemed so straightforward when we agreed to rent it for a month; now mysteries seem to be cropping up on all sides."

The other woman's voice took on a certain impressive dignity. "You are in my house, Miss Hollis; naturally I feel responsible. This man, whoever he may be, has no rights on the premises. I feel it my duty to see you have some protection."

"I've been in tricky situations before," Sarah insisted, "and this Oliver Abercrombie or whoever he really is doesn't seem to be hiding his light under a bushel. There can't be many men with American passports staying at St. Crécy. He could be found easily enough. It's not as though he can do me any harm; too many people know I'm here—you and Martin and the curé, and of course my friends in England." For some reason she couldn't have explained, she didn't mention Johnny.

"Accidents happen very easily," said the smooth voice. And Sarah found herself remembering the mysterious behavior of the little red car. "Martin will not only be protection for you; he will safeguard my interests also. I do not like the idea of this intruder hanging about my house."

"I suppose there couldn't be some mistake?" offered Sarah hopefully. "I mean, there have been cases of men reading their own obituaries. What I'm trying to say is that perhaps Oliver doesn't know yet that he's dead."

But that brought no adequate response. "I must implore you to lock the doors tonight; after that it will not matter, since Martin will be with you and he can be trusted to take care of things."

Abruptly the caller hung up. Sarah to her surprise found she was shivering a little. For the first time she began to wonder if the erratic behavior of her car had been due to accident and if it was sheer coincidence that Oliver Abercrombie—in lieu of another name, that was how she thought of him—should turn up at the villa immediately afterward.

The next day was Market Day, another blazing morning, though at last there was a refreshing breeze. Looking from her bedroom window at the superb view, refreshed by a night of dreamless sleep, Sarah felt as though yesterday itself—the latter part of it anyway—was no more than a dream. Only the letter she had begun to Pat and Polly bore testimony to Oliver's existence and proved he wasn't a figment of her imagination. After his departure she had added a paragraph, recording her meetings first with Johnny and then with the "intruder."

But whoever he is he won't try and break in, now he knows

the villa's occupied, she assured herself. All the same, it was a little disconcerting to realize how many unused rooms the house contained, and an enterprising villain could probably effect an entry during her absence. Only—why? She kept coming back to that question. Unless she was going to start believing the legend about hidden treasure, there seemed no conceivable reason why Oliver should trouble himself to call again. He'll meet his match in Martin, she decided, as she set about getting breakfast.

She made coffee and drank it black, reminding herself to inquire about possible milk delivery. Polly drank milk by the gallon. She toasted some bread, got out the car and sailed scornfully through the water-splash. The Market was held at St. Crécy, and she looked about her eagerly for some sign of Oliver, but she saw none. There were three or four smallish hotels here, and she fought down an impulse to go in and make inquiries. If he was on some illicit business it would be the most foolish thing she could do. Besides, she needed food, and all the best goods would be sold if she delayed further. The Market was a much more comprehensive affair than she had anticipated. It was held in a big covered hall, already packed with shoppers. She had to fight her way through the crowds. Women stood suspiciously regarding great heaps of colored vegetables, poking and prodding; other, equally suspicious, watched them from the farther side.

The haggling that went on was an entertainment in itself. Shrugged shoulders, raised voices, bargaining, cries of disbelief, screams of protest, all echoed back from the roof and walls. Sarah knew she couldn't hope to attain a Frenchwoman's skill, but at least, she told herself, she wouldn't be fleeced like some little English baa-lamb. She bought fruit and cheese and a long stiff loaf like a policeman's baton that wouldn't fit into any of her baskets. Later she saw some of the experienced peasants riding away on their bicycles, the loaf sticking up behind their backs like the tail of some very erect cat. She saw joints of meat of a shape and color she had never known; she bought sausage and pâté, unsalted French butter and dried fish; she paid an exorbitant price for something that was called veal—and, in fact, that was just what it was.

Outside there were other stalls unconnected with food. Tied to a pole were brilliantly colored bouffant petticoats blowing in the bright wind; colored umbrellas, scarfs, painted jugs and glasses. She bought a dish shaped like a fish intended for the oven, then moved on to look with enchantment at flowers that might have been brought that morning from paradise. She examined trays of vivid-colored sweets, few of them hygienically wrapped, and hurried back, her arms laden, to deposit the purchases in her car. She bought a white and gold silk scarf, two cartons of strong French cigarettes and some black-stemmed matches with pink heads.

All this time she saw no one she knew. She had wondered if perhaps she would glimpse the curé, but no doubt he was occupied in his parish. His housekeeper—even an impoverished French curé must have someone to look after him—might be any one of these busy, intent women, shopping so thriftily, probably despising her for being a tourist. She came away, enthralled by the morning's activities. Just beyond the market she saw a shop with postcards and stamps, and stopped to get some.

Returning through St. Mariole she identified Le Chat Qui Rit, which proved to be little more than a wineshop, with men sitting about outside at little tables, drinking wine or French beer. One thing, she told herself, Mrs. Abercrombie can never have stayed there; I doubt if they even take guests. Still, the sight of it reminded her that she had no wine and, seeing one or two men emerge carrying bottles, she stopped the car and went hardily in.

"I am staying at the Villa Abercrombie," she volunteered, waiting for change. There seemed no harm in letting as many people as possible know of her existence. But her statement elicited no interest. Two or three of the men regarded her with barefaced curiosity, and she met their gaze with candor. Let them stare, they'd know her again if—if anything went wrong. Not that it would, of course. At the farther end of the village she identified Monsieur Binet's garage and stopped once more for gas. A woman was in charge of the pumps and to her also Sarah volunteered the information that she was staying at the haunted villa. But once again the remark drew no response. If Oliver had asked his way it hadn't been here, and anyway a car like his would attract attention. If he was on a criminal expedition, it would be asking for trouble to make inquiries where he couldn't conceivably be overlooked.

As she threw in the clutch, Johnny himself appeared from the back, where he'd been working on a car.

"So you're still alive," he said cheerfully. "No ghoulies or ghosties?"

"I wouldn't go so far as to say that," she assured him. "I took a peep into some of the empty rooms today; you could hide an army there. As for the attics, they may be stiff with corpses."

"You make my mouth water. I've always longed to see a haunted chateau. Even a villa with a problematical ghost would be a start."

"Come tonight," she offered on impulse. "I've got masses to tell you. I suppose you're not a mystery writer in disguise?"

"I'm keeping that for my old age. Just at the moment I'd sooner have the adventures than record them."

"You'd get 'em all right if you wore my shoes. Never a dull moment. Strange men dropping in . . ."

"What did I tell you, Lorelei?"

"Risen from the grave to claim their rights, according to the record," she continued. "Forged passports, the lot."

"All this and the ghost, too? That's an irresistible combination. I can hardly wait."

"Then why not accept my invitation for tonight?"

"Why not indeed? Old Moneybags keeps me at it till eight, but I can come straight on after that."

"I'll be expecting you. I bought the fatted calf, at least a piece of him, in the market. By the way, don't be put off by the water-splash."

"They thought of everything, didn't they?" His voice sounded admiring. "No need for a bodyguard . . ."

"I'm getting one, whether I want one or not. Mrs. Abercrombie insists on Martin coming back—she rang me last night from Biarritz to make sure all was well."

"That was nice of her. Speaking personally, I'd have thought you were safer without that randy old goat."

"You told me yourself he has his homework in the neighborhood," Sarah reminded him.

"Chaps like Martin are gluttons for overtime. Just as well, I should think, if I do come up. Matter of fact, if you're interested, I could tell you quite a lot about that household. I take it you haven't met Marie? She's the one who wears the trousers. Probably Martin married her for her father's dowry and her expectations, whatever they may be."

"The hidden treasure!" she said triumphantly. "You're as gossipy as an old maid."

"Ah, but I've had no one to gossip with for so long. You just mention the villa to any of the locals and they start crossing themselves."

"Then they must be a very pagan lot at Le Chat Qui Rit. I didn't see any crossings going on there when I mentioned it."

"No spitting?"

"Not that I noticed."

"Probably waited till you were out of sight. What were you doing there?"

"Buying wine."

"That explains it. They wouldn't want to antagonize the landlady, proprietress, whatever she calls her. Mère Angelique—people do have the most unsuitable names, don't they? I must say, I wish I'd met the old one—Miss Abercrombie. The present owner is probably wax in the Ribauds' hands."

"I'd say this one had been getting the better of people for about twenty years in Paris," Sarah assured him. "She and

(55)

Marie must be wrastle, gouge and rabbit punch all along the line." Only of course it was different with Martin.

"Are we talking about the same woman?" murmured Johnny politely. "By the way, did you give any further thought to what might have happened to your car?"

"We know what happened. A nut worked itself loose."

"If you say so. Hullo, here's old Moneybags himself." He broke into a spate of French directions. Then when Sarah had driven off with a final murmured, "Tonight then?" he stood gazing after the little red car.

5

Sarah, merry as a grig, drove back to the villa and put away her purchases. The realization that Johnny would be visiting that evening gave her a sense of something more than satisfaction, a kind of exhilaration. Perhaps tonight she might tell him in greater detail about last night's telephone call. She surveyed the meat she had bought and decided that with plenty of vegetables it would look handsome enough for two. She sampled the cheese, which was excellent, and also the sausage. During the afternoon there was a sharp burst of rain. I should have realized it was too clear for the fine weather to last, she told herself, as she ran to put the little car into the garage. At about three o'clock the telephone rang once more, and she went to answer it with a sense of lively anticipation. Who would it be this time? Oliver? Martin, announcing the time of his arrival? Or Johnny, saying he'd changed his mind? Not, she hoped, the last. But in point of fact it was none of these. When she lifted the receiver the voice that came over the line was one she had never heard before.

"The Villa Abercrombie?" it said, speaking a foreigner's

English. "Is that Miss Hollis? *Bonjour, mademoiselle.* This is Marie Ribaud. I should like, if you please, to speak to my husband."

"He's not here," said Sarah. "Not yet, that is. I told Mrs. Abercrombie there was no need for him to break up his holiday; I'm perfectly all right."

The woman's voice sounded bewildered. "Mrs. Abercrombie . . . ?"

"She rang through from Biarritz last night, and—but didn't you know? I mean—I thought your husband was joining you after depositing Mrs. Abercrombie at Biarritz. You didn't know?" Quickly she outlined the situation. "I do see it's all rather complicated," she agreed. "I suppose the fact is they reached Biarritz so late that he had to stay the night there and he couldn't get in touch with you, so really it's a good thing you rang up. You must have been worried when he didn't arrive, if you were expecting him," she added, this aspect of the case suddenly occurring to her.

"It was arranged that he should remain until your arrival. I supposed—which day was it that you came?"

"Tuesday. My telegram didn't get delivered the right day, which explains the confusion. I just said tomorrow, which was silly of me. All the same . . ." She stopped, frowning, perplexed in her turn. "I was thinking—even if he had to spend Tuesday night at Biarritz, he should have joined you yesterday. And Mrs. Abercrombie didn't say he was there. I suppose he would be coming by car?"

"Yes, mademoiselle." The voice was quite toneless now.

"I was thinking—they had a flat tire on the way to the station; that's why he had to drive her all the way to Biarritz —what I mean is, the car could have broken down."

But she spoke lamely; she was remembering Mrs. Abercrombie's attitude toward Martin, not at all what you would expect of a smart Parisian toward her chauffeur-gardener, which was really what he was. There's some mystery here, she thought, and felt gladder than ever that Johnny was coming tonight.

"If you will give me a number where I can reach you—a telephone number, I mean—I'll get him to ring as soon as he arrives," she promised. "In the meantime, don't worry." She waited for some response, but all she heard was the click of the telephone as Marie replaced the receiver.

"Curiouser and curiouser," she quoted, going back to the kitchen, where she was planning an elaborate dessert for her guest. "What was it Pat said? That she hoped I'd manage to pass the time till they arrived? She doesn't know. Never a dull moment."

Absorbedly she began breaking eggs into a bowl.

Marie Ribaud came out of the bistro where she had been telephoning and walked blindly back to her son-in-law's bakery a few doors away. She was a short, sturdy figure, giving out an aura of darkness. Auguste, her son-in-law, on the other hand, was as pink and bouncing as one of his own sugar buns. Even a permanently tearful wife, convinced she would die with the birth of her child, did little to depress his spirits. When he saw Marie's face, however, his own expression changed.

"What is it, *belle-mère*?" He led her into the little parlor—Celline, his wife, was lying down upstairs—and poured out a small glass of wine. "You have bad news?"

Marie took the wine and sipped it as though she did not realize what she was doing. Her little black hat threw a shade over features that were now as white as cheese. Her eyes, round and black like the eyes of a mouse or a canary, stared blankly into his.

"It is Martin?" coaxed Auguste, who didn't fancy two drooping women on his hands. "Something is wrong?"

He knew his father-in-law had been expected the day before, but he also knew about Martin's roving temperament—knew and sympathized. The circumstances of life at the villa gave him few opportunities for pleasure outside the thorny bonds of matrimony to a woman as cozy as a hedgehog.

Doubtless he had his interests outside the home, and this was a rare chance to indulge them.

"It is the young English girl at the Villa Abercrombie," Marie explained. "She says that she met Madame leaving just as she herself arrived. Martin was to drive her to the station. But, Auguste, Martin drove us both into Pau on Tuesday morning, where Madame left for Biarritz and I caught the train to come to you—so who was it that Miss Hollis saw at the villa on Tuesday night?"

Auguste was a man of quick reactions. He refilled the glass Marie had unconsciously emptied and said, "Perhaps Madame found she had forgotten her passport and returned."

"Her passport was in her bag. I saw it myself. No, Auguste, it is *impossible* that Miss Hollis should have seen Madame that night."

Auguste shrugged. "Some friend perhaps, someone to help Martin to prepare the villa for the young lady. You said she came before she was expected."

"Why should he tell Miss Hollis it was Mrs. Abercrombie?"

"Perhaps she assumed it and there was no time to enter into explanations."

"Then where is Martin now? Or do you suggest he is *walking* from Biarritz?"

The shop bell pinged and Auguste went to attend to a customer. Marie remained motionless, her thoughts as dark as a stormy night. She could read her son-in-law's mind; he thought Martin was with another woman, though not Mrs. Abercrombie. For once she found herself in agreement with him.

Sarah, unaware of the gathering storm, continued her preparations for her first invited guest. Oliver had come unasked, so he didn't count. "Count?" Crook was to say a bit later. "Don't they teach girls arithmetic at these posh schools they go to?"

Even after the shower of rain she didn't dare risk a second

bath in twenty-four hours, but splashed like a canary in the basin. Then she put on a dress in turquoise blue linen bought especially for the holiday, added earrings and a necklace of blue beads she had brought back from Venice, brushed her pale gold hair till it shone. When she saw the eager face looking back at her from the glass, she thought reproachfully, You don't look very broken-hearted; I hope you're not going to prove fickle. But she reminded herself that everything had proceeded at such a rush she hadn't had time to think about Simon. When she had, the pain of course would return. The little gilt bells jingled in her ears as she ran down to the kitchen and peeped into the oven. She decanted wine, set out drinks, opened a tin of crackers, a jar of olives, a fresh pack of cigarettes. Good enough for a woman's magazine, she told herself: all the ingredients for a three-parter—mysterious setting, heroine, villain—and what a smiling villain! Now they awaited the hero. The sun's gone to your head, she told herself; you better watch out. She didn't know then that she had cautioned herself too late.

The bell rang earlier than she had anticipated but it didn't matter, because everything was ready. She ran to the door, but there was no one there.

"Where are you, Johnny?" she called, and the bell pealed again. "You've gone to the wrong door," she cried, laughing, and came running gaily around the corner of the house to bring him in.

It was the oldest trick in the world. Something caught her under the knees. She stumbled, flung out an arm to save herself and came sprawling. As she scrambled up, an arm came around her neck from behind; her head was jerked back against a rough cloth shoulder.

"Are you mad?" she spluttered, struggling to free herself. "I said drinks, not . . ." A hand closed over her mouth; twisting, she saw her visitor's face.

"You!" she whispered, but no sound came. "You!"

"You were warned," said her visitor. "Why can't you listen to good advice? You've only yourself to blame."

(61)

The palm over her mouth was like a padlock. Then, without warning, the darkness came down like a curtain, though she was scarcely aware of a blow. Her assailant smiled. It had all been too easy. And, after all, events had proved him right. She had been warned, but she wouldn't heed the warning. You might say she had no one but herself to blame.

6

Monsieur le Curé was enjoying an excellent Breton stew when his doorbell rang, and he heard his housekeeper stump along the hall to answer it. Eugénie—and what an unsuitable name that was!—was short, stout and bulging-eyed like a frog. She was an excellent housekeeper and an even better cook, and she guarded him more fiercely than any wife could have done. He heard the door open and a moment later her indignant voice, clearly denying someone entry.

It is a good thing, the curé reflected, that *le bon Dieu* did not consider her in the role of the Recording Angel; heaven would remain empty throughout eternity. Sadly he pushed his plate aside and rose. On the doorstep Eugénie was trying to fend off a stubborn young man who looked as much like a battering ram as any human creature could.

"You tell him he'll be an accessory after the crime if he doesn't see me," the visitor was storming, speaking French in the manner of one to whom it is a second tongue.

"What crime is that, monsieur?" inquired the priest, moving down the narrow hall.

"I don't know exactly," acknowledged the young man, "but it could be murder."

The curé was peering through the shadows of the passage. Eugénie's housekeeping included the most frugal of lights. "It is the young Englishman from the garage, is it not?"

"That's right. Johnny Bryce. Monsieur le Curé, there's something very fishy going on at the Villa Abercrombie. You knew an English girl had arrived?"

The curé smiled, remembering with pleasure that unexpected encounter. "I met her; she had lost her way."

"It looks now as if she may have lost it permanently," Johnny told him grimly. "I was due to have a meal there tonight—eight o'clock, she said—and she was going to tell me something—I feel it—but there was no time for details. You know what Monsieur Binet's like. He not only wants his pound of flesh; he wants an extra ounce thrown in. We couldn't talk at the garage earlier. I've just been to the villa and—what do you think? The whole place is locked up like a prison—or a grave—and there's a notice VILLA FERMÉE on the gate."

"The young lady has changed her mind," said Eugénie emphatically.

"She's not a weathercock," Johnny objected. "And if she wanted to cancel our arrangement she only had to telephone. I told her the number. No, someone's out to get her. I suspected it when I saw what had happened to her car; that nut never loosened itself." He explained how the car had gone out of control.

The curé coaxed him into his study, sent Eugénie for wine and suggested that Johnny start at the beginning.

"There's no time," protested Johnny desperately. "Every minute could make a difference."

"If you are setting out on a race it is helpful to know in which direction you should run," said the curé in his calm way. When Eugénie, looking as black as a crow, came back with the wine and two glasses, the curé sent her for a third.

"Eugénie may be able to help us here," he remarked.

"Eugénie, the young lady from the Villa Abercrombie—you have seen her?"

"I suppose that would be her in the Market," scowled Eugénie. "It is no wonder the British have a national debt. No Frenchwoman would pay the prices she paid—just think of it, for a bunch of grapes no bigger than sultanas . . ."

"Monsieur Bryce has been to the villa," interrupted the curé ruthlessly. "The gates are locked, like a fortress, and yet he went by invitation."

"Perhaps mademoiselle is afraid of being alone."

"But she wouldn't be alone—not with me," exclaimed Johnny. "Besides, she's not that kind. It's not as though I were a stranger; I'd been there before. And if she thought she was in danger she only had to say the word. And she certainly wouldn't have put up that notice. The point is why? Why?"

"Did you notice, monsieur, if the car was still there?" the curé inquired.

Johnny considered. "I suppose it was in the garage." Suddenly he paled. "No, I didn't think of the car." It was an old story, familiarized by films and detective yarns, and occasionally heard in the coroner's court. You pushed your victim, inside his or her car, into the garage; you switched on the engine and locked the door. And then you went and bought yourself a drink or took a girl to bed. When the body was found the verdict was death from carbon monoxide poisoning, and if you were lucky the jury found a verdict of suicide, probably while of unsound mind. Only—not in this case.

"I'm going in," said Johnny, his mouth dry. "If I have to break down the gate I'm going in."

"Finish your wine, my son," said the curé.

Eugénie turned angrily on the young man. "Why do you have to come here to ruin Monsieur le Curé's digestion?" she screeched, like a hen peacock. "What harm has he done you, he who does only good to all? If you consider something is wrong, there are the police, *n'est-ce pas*? This is a matter for them." She glared impartially at both men.

"Police!" repeated Johnny derisively. "*Ce pauvre saucisson!*"

he exclaimed, remembering the old bumbling gendarme at the station at St. Mariole. "I doubt if he's arrested anything larger than a straying hen in ten years. You know his rule, do everything by the book. I tell you, there's no time. I'm going in."

Eugénie stamped out. "Another dinner wasted," she said.

"My son," the curé told his visitor, "you cannot expect the police to break down a gate on no more evidence than you can show them."

"The rest of the evidence will be on the other side of the wall," Johnny prophesied grimly. "And I'm not asking the police to do anything. You've both assured me it would be a waste of time."

"How would you think?" the curé inquired, in the same mild voice. "A young man comes in with just such a story. Ho-ho, they would laugh, here is a young English lady who fears a visit from a man; she plays him like a fish; come, she says, come tonight, come when your work is done; and then back she flies, she packs, she leaves."

"Carefully padlocking the gate and putting out a label before she goes? It doesn't make sense, monsieur, and anyway she's not that sort of girl."

"Or perhaps, they will say, she is sitting behind a curtain laughing at the same young man, never having left the premises."

"Or not laughing, because she can't," suggested Johnny grimly. "Anyway, she's not that sort, she wouldn't think it funny. She asked me because she wanted me to come, and she meant to be there when I arrived. Only—someone else, don't ask me who, didn't intend us to meet. And don't ask me why. My guess is she knows something, whether she herself realizes it or not, that makes her a danger. Oh, I know that sounds melodramatic, but life is melodramatic sometimes. So I'm going back now and I'll get inside the place, if I have to come down the chimney."

"And if you are apprehended by the police, having broken in?"

"I shall tell them the truth, that I was invited . . ."

"Did anyone hear mademoiselle invite you? Did you speak of it . . . ?"

"To old Binet? Not likely. And there's been no time to talk to anyone else. And since we were talking English it's not likely anyone would have understood if we had been overheard. I don't understand your attitude," he wound up bluntly. "I thought you'd want to help."

"Consider, my son. If you wished to break into the house—and you would not be the first since the old lady's death—what better story could you tell? A story you cannot hope to prove . . ."

"You're forgetting the alleged accident to the car, aren't you, monsieur? That was no accident. I'm the expert. I know."

"You spoke to Monsieur Binet of the accident perhaps?"

"If I'd told that whey-faced old codger I'd helped to put it right, he'd have sent a bill. If I'd told anyone else, he would have said, 'Nice going, boy. Don't waste time, do you? I suppose she hasn't got a girl friend? We might make up a foursome.' No, I didn't tell anyone." His young face, tanned by the sun, was dark with anger.

"And yet for a girl about whom you know nothing—well, practically nothing—you are prepared to commit a felony. I believe breaking into a house after dark is burglary."

"Only if you take something from it. Yes, I mean to do just that. Sarah's got to be somewhere. Of course, whoever locked the villa and left the note on the gate could have taken her away with him, but it's not so easy concealing an English girl in a small French village."

"And you think perhaps she did not leave the house?"

"I certainly intend to find out."

"But since the gates are padlocked . . ."

"Hillary climbed higher things than an iron gate when he went up Everest," Johnny reminded him. "Besides, there are trees, and I can get some leverage from my bike."

"Where precisely do you propose to make this felonious entry?"

"Wherever it's most convenient. One thing, at this time of the evening no one's likely to see me . . ."

"But if you were to be seen by some respectable citizen making an illegal entry, it would be that citizen's duty to summon the police. However, by the time anyone arrived you would have had opportunity enough to answer your first question—whether the young lady is still on the premises. Had you wondered how you would enter the villa itself?"

"There aren't many windows that can stand up to a healthy boot. At least, I can find out if the car's still there. If it isn't, that puts a different complexion on things."

"You realize that by telling me this you are making me an accessory before the crime?"

"You try stopping me," offered Johnny.

"I am an old man, but still I know my duty. What you are proposing is against the law; it is my duty to report offenses of which I have knowledge."

"Go right ahead," Johnny invited him. "Only, give me ten minutes, say fifteen, before you pick up your phone and ring up that *pauvre saucisson*."

"I happen to know the *pauvre saucisson* is suffering from a quinsy. No, the word must go through to St. Crécy. It so happens that my brother Louis is a sergeant there . . ."

"And you'd ring him."

"If I were convinced you were in earnest, that would be my duty."

"I suppose he has a car. Well, I'd back my motorcycle against any French car six days out of seven. Still, best give me fifteen minutes to be on the safe side."

"You are forgetting," the curé rebuked him, "that I myself travel on a bicycle."

"You mean—you're coming yourself?" Johnny sounded staggered.

"How can I give first-hand evidence of a misdemeanor—and that is the only kind of evidence my brother, the sergeant, will be prepared to accept—unless I have seen for myself? Besides," he added, smiling that gentle smile, "getting over the wall may be more difficult than you suppose."

"Blow me down!" said Johnny in reverent tones. "You're on our side. O.K., monsieur, get your hat, we're off to the races. I tell you, chaps have been canonized for less."

After Johnny had gone storming off on his motorcycle the curé shouted for his housekeeper. "Eugénie, I have to go out immediately," he announced.

"I knew it," the woman grumbled. "Why I trouble to cook . . ."

"We are only required to do our duty," the curé reminded her. He had the maddening qualities of all would-be saints. "What follows is not our concern. My bicycle . . ."

"I think I noticed a puncture."

"Then I must ride it on the rim." Like Arthur Crook, whom he was so soon to meet, he had all the answers.

Down the road he sailed, like some gaunt bird of ill omen. One of these days, doubtless, he would fall off and one of these murderous cars, driven by an *anglais,* would run him down. And that would be the end of him, an inglorious end to a man of God who should die decently in his bed, fortified by the rites of Holy Church.

The young Englishman was certainly a person of enterprise, the curé reflected, as he came bumping down the stony lane on his ancient bicycle. Halfway down the lane he saw Johnny's motorcycle leaning against the wall, and when he rang his own rusty bell the young man's head popped up from the other side.

"You'd better get hold of your brother, monsieur," he observed in grim tones. "Sarah was expecting me all right, drinks laid out, and the dinner keeping hot in the oven. Lucky in a way the house hasn't gone up in smoke. No sign of her, though the car's still in the garage."

"The door is unlocked?" The curé sounded dubious.

"Not likely. I went in through a window—Johnny Bryce, the human projectile. It's an incredible house—one locked room, but I don't think that has any significance. One thing, she didn't take any luggage, her bags are in one of the rooms, and all her bits and pieces—you know, things like toothbrushes and sponge, the lot—they're all there. Well, your reverence, is that enough to get the local police away from their game of *boule*?"

"You are sure there is no one here? Guard yourself well, my son."

The curé remounted his ramshackle bicycle and pedaled full tilt back to the presbytery.

7

Sergeant Louis Grasse was preparing to call it a day and go off duty when he was told that his brother Jean was asking for him urgently on the telephone. Immediately the anticipatory smile was wiped from his face, to be replaced by a scowl. Jean on the line, in the sergeant's experience, invariably spelled trouble. He picked up the receiver and listened, the scowl deepening with every word the curé said.

"You seriously suggest I shall take men off duty because you saw some *gamin* bird's-nesting in the grounds of an empty villa? The poor fool can't know the owner's reputation well if he imagines she would leave so much as an egg unblown in the nest before her departure."

"I do not think he is a *gamin,* Louis, nor do I think he is bird's-nesting. He rode a motorcycle; he had a most resolute air. Nor can he be described as a boy. I tell you, I myself saw him scramble over the wall."

"What were you doing in the lane at that hour?" his brother demanded suspiciously. "You admit yourself Madame is away . . ."

"I followed the young man. I was curious to know why a motorcycle should be turning into the lane at this hour of the evening. As we know, it leads nowhere but to the villa. And that is closed."

"I thought I heard it had been let to an English party."

The curé made a rapid volte-face. "Who will have any respect for our French law if we allow trespassers to break in, and do nothing? Louis, if you do not intend to pursue this case, then I am bound to warn you it will be a dereliction of duty, and to refrain from performing one's duty is a sin."

He hung up the receiver, and once again rang for the long-suffering Eugénie. "My brother Louis, the *sergent de ville,* has had a report of a crime in this parish," he announced blandly. (Crook would have called him a police constable.)

"Then let him get on with his work and leave you to yours," retorted the dauntless old woman.

"Nevertheless, since it was I who laid the information . . ."

"You! It was the young *anglais,* of course?"

"Everything he told me is true. I have myself been to the villa. The young lady has vanished."

"Gone out for a drive, I daresay."

"I do not think so. Her car is in the garage. I tell you this under the seal," he added firmly. "No talking, Eugénie." No one knew better than the curé that you can't put the members of your congregation under the seal in such circumstances, but it was a trick that never failed. "I have done my duty; now see to it that you do yours."

"Can't keep out of anything," grumbled Eugénie. "You'll see, Monsieur le Curé, if there's any credit to be had, they'll take it. And you know very well the sergeant won't want you there," she added shrewdly.

The curé knew this only too well. His one hope of remaining in the picture was to get to the villa ahead of the police, and once there refuse to budge. Otherwise, curé or no, brother or no, he'd find the door slammed in his face. Looking more than ever like some ancient, noble bird, he returned down the road. Once out of sight of his presbytery he abandoned all attempts at dignity and pedaled like mad. Before reaching the turn to the villa, he heard the sound of wheels coming up behind him. He had no doubt at all what this meant; the police car was beating him in the race. But he was not so easily defeated.

Instead of drawing to the side of the road and allowing the car to pass him, he clung obstinately to the crown, wavering this way and that so that it would be positively dangerous to try and get by. The driver hooted furiously; Jean affably rang his bell in response. He was going so fast he almost overran the mouth of the lane, and swerved so sharply that a less experienced man, or one even a shade less resolute, would have been thrown off. In the lane itself he had more excuse for proceeding with caution and keeping to the middle of the road; nevertheless, the pair of them—the crazy curé and his lunatic bicycle, bumped and flew with the car hooting in his ear. Turning a corner, he saw the motorcycle still propped against the wall, and at last made way for the police.

"He is still here," he pointed out gratuitously to the sergeant.

"We should have found that out without our help," his brother Louis informed him ungraciously. "There was no need for you to accompany us. We can deal with one young lawbreaker on our own account."

"I have just recalled," said Jean blandly, "that there was a young lady—I met her, on Tuesday it would be—she asked the way to the villa. You see what that means? If she is alone she may be in danger."

"You are sure it was a young lady you beheld, and not a heavenly vision?" inquired Louis with immense irony. "It would not be the first time a man of your cloth was vouchsafed a sight of the Virgin Mary . . ."

"I never heard Our Blessed Lady spoke English, and indeed why should she learn so barbarous a language? This was a young English lady. She was seen at the market this morning by Eugénie. Does that sound as though she intended to return to her own country? And yet there is a notice on the gate: VILLA FERMÉE."

The sergeant seemed half choked with indignation. "I warn you, Jean," he said, "if you have brought us out on a wild-goose chase, it will be the worse for you. And now, should your assistance be required you will be informed. Any attempt to follow my men into the grounds will be regarded as a matter of trespass."

He indicated to two of the gendarmes who had accompanied him that they should follow the young Englishman's example and scale the wall.

"You see," said Jean persuasively, "you are not altogether without faith, Louis. A true unbeliever would make certain that the gates are padlocked."

He watched the policemen disappear. Johnny had prudently remained hidden; he at all events intended to remain in the heart of the picture. As soon as the police were over the wall the curé shot down the hill.

"What's the old goat up to now?" the driver of the police car wondered. The curé disappeared from sight around a curve in the lane. As he had assured Sarah, there was a pedestrian crossing by the water-splash in the shape of a rough log bridge. This he crossed and vanished into a thicket of small bushes and tall, savage nettles. One advantage of being the local priest was a private view, as it were, of local opportunities for wrongdoing. More than one of his penitents had confessed to breaking into the grounds during the old woman's lifetime through a man-made—and carefully concealed—gap where the wall was weak. They were lured partly by the knowledge that she grew luxuries like peaches —this was an error but it persisted—and asparagus in the garden, which could be sold for a price, and, after her death, by the rumor of gold hidden there. Once through the gap, the curé set off in the direction of lights and voices, and was part of the group around the villa before anyone had noticed his arrival.

As he entered the drawing room, where the company was assembled, the first thing he heard was Johnny's voice exclaiming, "Surely that's proof positive she didn't go of her own free will. No girl goes out without her handbag."

As the curé joined them his brother looked up and his face darkened, as though he had seen the devil, whom he possibly would have preferred.

"I gave instructions," he began, but Jean said, "I promised mademoiselle to come to her assistance if harm should befall her. You would not have me break that promise."

"By invoking the law you have fulfilled your promise," declared Sergeant Louis Grasse pompously, but, if he wasn't pleased to see his brother, Johnny welcomed the curé with open arms.

"You'll back me up," he declared. "You know that a girl wouldn't just disappear and leave her bag behind. Girls won't stir a step without their make-up."

"Louis," said the curé "is the passport there?" His voice was as grave as a funeral march.

The sergeant zipped open a side pocket and out it slid, the slender dark-blue document issued in the name of Her Britannic Majesty, requesting succor and protection for the holder from the authorities of all the countries through which she might pass. As Louis Grasse opened the book a card slid to the ground. Johnny stooped to retrieve it.

"Arthur Crook!" he said, reading it aloud. "Wonder where on earth she ran across him. It takes wild bulls—or a job—to make him cross the Channel. He's a lawyer from London," he added for the benefit of his audience, "and, believe me, he's the works."

Louis held out his hand for the card; turning it over he saw an address on the back. Hotel Collioure, Bordeaux.

The curé looked more distressed than before. "Monsieur Bryce is right," he said. "Something is amiss."

"That damned stranger!" ejaculated Johnny.

"Crimes," continued the curé, as though proceeding from one point in a sermon to the next, "are normally committed for one of two reasons, from greed or from fear. In this case the motive is hardly likely to be greed. So far as you have ascertained nothing has been taken, there is no sign that the villa has been searched, and in any case what could a young

English girl have that would have been of such value as to justify this violent step? So—it is fear."

"And who," capped his brother, "is likely to be afraid of this same young English girl, who has only been among us for two or three days?"

"My dear brother, when we know the answer to that we shall have the answer to the whole question. Possibly she has stumbled on some inconvenient truth. Truth has always been an expensive commodity. All through the ages it has been the price of blood." He caught sight of Johnny's face and hurried on, "You have, of course, heard the legend of concealed treasure, dating back perhaps to the day of old Monsieur Abercrombie, whom none of us remembers."

"Why don't we examine her room?" broke out Johnny. "If she hasn't taken any luggage it must be obvious she was decoyed away. That is, if the bag and the passport themselves aren't sufficient evidence to convince you."

The sergeant and his men departed on a tour of investigation. Johnny turned to the priest.

"What do you think, *mon père*?"

"I do not like the passport being found," the curé allowed. Many things that are regarded as necessities are found to be expendable at times of emergencies, but papers—without papers nowadays a person has no identity. They are virtually his license to live. Yes, my son, I am afraid for the young lady. And there is another thing. If whoever is responsible—let us call him X—had not been in a great hurry, he would have looked for the bag. It is, I think, safe to presume that he was surprised into making what is called a getaway, perhaps hoping to return later."

Johnny groaned. "The chap who scared him must have been me. No one else would have a reason to come to the villa tonight. Heard the sound of my motorbike, I daresay. Why, he could have been no more than a stone's throw away while I stood by the gate reading his damned notice. All he'd have to do was retreat along the lane round the bend and wait for me to leave."

"When he would take advantage of his opportunity to do likewise?"

"I suppose he went by the mountain road. He'd hardly dare risk coming through the village. Let's find out what's afoot in the rest of the house," he added.

The police were plodding through the villa like a pack of ponderous elderly terriers examining a rabbit hole. Here was none of the excited yelping of young dogs, but a stolid movement from stage to stage. It was easy to identify the room Sarah had chosen for herself, it had already taken on the identity of youth. A few wild flowers stood in a glass on the dressing table; open wardrobe doors revealed an array of crisp, bright dresses; a toilet bag in flowered white plastic with a jaunty little frill hung over the back of a chair. A faint scent of powder and perfume hung about the air. At any moment you expected a door to burst open and the girl herself to come dancing in. Nothing of the kind, of course, happened.

"I'll tell you one thing," said Johnny suddenly. "She'd changed her dress. That's the one she was wearing this morning." He indicated a candy-striped cotton now neatly resting on its hanger. "I remember particularly because it reminded me of my mother's new bathroom wallpaper."

"There is a locked door here, Sergeant," said one of the gendarmes. "Do we break it down?"

"If it is necessary. But first try two or three room keys. One of them may fit."

The second key they tried opened the door smoothly enough. The room into which they all surged was better furnished and more cheerful than the others they had seen. The curtains at the window were new and gaily patterned. There were scatter rugs, also new, on the shabby floor covering; cushions on the hard upright chairs. Bed, dressing table and a small writing desk had been covered with dust sheets. When these were removed they revealed precisely what might have been expected—dustless, polished surfaces. The dressing table showed a cloisonné powder box, a Regency china dish for rings and brooches. Brush, comb, cosmetics, all were missing. Louis pulled out the drawers, flung open the wardrobes. One or two warm dresses and a smart topcoat, neatly shrouded in garment bags, revealed themselves. There were shoes on a rack, but anything that might be useful for a holiday in a warm climate had disappeared. It was a simple task, too, to realize that this room housed no corpse, though the police were thorough enough in their search, peering under the bed, throwing the clothes out of the cupboards. They even looked up at the ceiling as if they thought they might find a secret trapdoor there, but it shone under a fresh coat of paint. That Madame had got her money's worth out of Martin was the thought that passed through the minds of both brothers.

"There is no secret here," Louis announced. "Madame departed as she had proclaimed."

"I could have told you that," said Johnny impatiently. "Sarah saw her go, with Martin, on Tuesday night, and on Wednesday Mrs. Abercrombie rang through from Biarritz—I suppose to make sure everything was all right. Their first meeting was such a rush. . . . What is it?" he broke off to inquire sharply of the curé.

"You are certain that Miss Hollis told you she had met Madame Abercrombie?"

"That's what I said."

"But Madame left Pau for Biarritz on Tuesday morning. I had that from Martin himself. He had driven her and Marie into Pau to catch their respective trains."

"She must have returned," said the sergeant briskly.

"I do not think so, Louis. We have been wondering why anyone should wish to harm Miss Hollis."

"We do not yet know . . ."

"Yes, we do," interrupted Johnny rudely. "There was the car." He explained about that. "And when I saw her at the garage she said something about a mysterious visitor with a forged passport. . . .Why should anyone want to get her off the premises, *mon père*?"

"We have no proof yet that she did not leave of her own will," insisted the sergeant.

"Leaving her bag—and passport? And the food in the oven? Besides, she'd changed her dress. I noticed the one she wore this morning. And that tells us something else. She wouldn't surely change until just before she expected me—that's to say, eight o'clock. Say seven at the earliest, which gives X an hour at most. And I'll tell you one thing more," he continued fluently, disregarding Louis's attempts to get a word in edgewise. "Whoever is responsible must have intended to come back and collect the passport, etc. Only I interrupted him, and he couldn't guess how long I'd be away. I might have gone for the police; he wouldn't dare wait. I suppose there's still a chance he might come back."

"If he does he will run straight into our arms," intoned the sergeant. "Naturally I shall leave a man on guard, inconvenient though it is. Who is this mysterious visitor of whom she spoke?"

"She was going to tell me tonight, but I fancy Mrs. Abercrombie had some ideas, because as soon as Sarah spoke of him, she—Mrs. A.—insisted on Martin coming back to protect her. It sounds as though she knew who he was."

In the meantime the search of the villa was continuing at the hands of the police. Neither Louis nor his brother could rule out the possibility that the girl was hidden somewhere in one of the attics, cupboards or cellars. Stumbling up the stairs, opening the doors of immense presses in empty rooms, peering behind rolls of disused linoleum and discarded furniture, testing the flags of the icy cellar, peering into outbuildings, the police went on, and all to no purpose. Sarah Hollis had disappeared like a wraith of dust.

"I do not think X will reappear," said the curé in exhausted tones. "The story of the murdered English girl will be all over St. Mariole by morning."

"Who is speaking of murder?" demanded Louis, though he must have known the thought was in every heart.

"Everyone will have a different version of the affair as

soon as it is known that the girl has vanished." The curé turned and the sergeant with him as the door of the room was pushed open and one of the searching gendarmes came in. They had looked everywhere, they declared; there was no trace.

"Is there a garden shed?" asked the curé and they stared. It appeared that there were two outbuildings which might be so described: one, falling into ruin, housed an ancient deed box (empty) and a covey of spiders and centipedal insects concealed beneath rotting planks; the other, of more recent origin, had been used by Martin to house garden tools. Without waiting for further comment the curé swept through the house and out by the back door.

"What do you expect to find that my men cannot see?" Louis demanded.

"I thought," said the curé in a low voice, "the tools might furnish a clue."

The tools looked like anybody else's—spade, gardening forks—one with dried mud adhering to the tines—rake, hoe and trowel; sticks for propping up peas, a handmower, a large wheelbarrow, a pair of muddy boots, rabbit wire and netting to preserve the fruit from the birds—and that was all. Nothing like a body. The curé spun the wheel of the upended barrow; here, too, a little mud clung and a fossilized yellow flower. The whole place was neat and well kept, the shed of a gardener who is careful of his implements. The curé turned away. There was nothing to help them here. Even if there had been time to dig a grave the mud on the fork, on the wheel of the barrow, was too hard, too old . . .

As they moved toward the house he said to his brother, "How many men are you able to spare for this matter, Louis?"

"I am not able to spare anyone," Louis snapped. "One man I have undertaken to leave . . ."

"You must find a second," insisted the curé firmly, "to guard the young Englishman." And, without being asked, he told the sergeant why.

As they came into the villa their attention was distracted by the clanging of a bell. It rang out as violently as a protest.

"Perhaps the young lady has changed her mind and decided to come back to us," suggested Louis disagreeably.

"Much more likely to be the press," said Johnny, overhearing him. "They seem to have a sixth sense for bad news."

But when one of the gendarmes went to open the gate he found a dark, gypsyish-looking man pawing as impatiently in the dust as any warhorse. When he saw the uniform he said, "What the hell goes on here? Madame sent me back to look after the English girl, she had some idea—what's the point in locking the gates?"

He shook them impatiently. "Open up, won't you?"

But the gendarme had no key. Martin ran along the side of the wall to the weak place where the curé had already made an entrance. As he came into the garden the front door opened and two figures appeared, black against the light that streamed feebly from the hall. Martin recognized the sergeant and scowled. Then he saw the curé and groaned. If the police spelled trouble, in Martin's opinion the Church spelled twice as much. "What's he doing here?" he muttered.

The curé came down to meet him in long, swooping steps. "*Bon soir,* Martin," he said. "Now perhaps we can proceed with our inquiries."

His brother unceremoniously shoved him aside. "You are Martin Ribaud and you work at the villa? We are anxious about the English girl who arrived on Tuesday evening."

"I only know Madame sent me back—something about a man calling himself Oliver Abercrombie who, she thought, might be dangerous to the girl. What Marie is going to say . . . Madame wanted her to go to some pension until we were due to return, but the English never listen to reason." He seemed thoroughly out of temper. "Where is she now?"

"Mademoiselle Hollis? She has disappeared."

"She's been abducted," interrupted Johnny.

Martin stared at him. "Where do you come in?"

"I will ask the questions," announced the sergeant. "Who is this Oliver Abercrombie?"

"He was the son of old Madame's brother, who went to America many years ago, before Marie and I ever heard the name of Abercrombie. When the lawyer advertised for an heir he was told that this Oliver had been killed in a car accident—details of the funeral were sent—so Madame Abercrombie from Paris inherited. She has no idea who this man might be . . ."

Inevitably the curé proceeded to make difficulties. "It does not occur to you he is perhaps the man he claims to be? It would not be the first time a man has read of his own death in the papers."

Martin shrugged. "It seems funny to me. Why not go to the lawyer in the first place? But perhaps he thought the villa would be empty."

"Don't tell me," said Johnny. "He'd heard about the treasure and came to investigate."

Martin's face turned black with anger. "You can laugh," he said, "but we have had trouble enough about this treasure. It seems strange that everyone should know about it except Marie and me. We lived here with the old woman all those years, and she never spoke of it."

"The legend persists," put in the curé in his steady voice.

Martin was forced to agree. "The beggars who've come calling since the old woman died—they didn't come in her lifetime, she had no charity for them. It was no wonder Madame wouldn't be left here alone; always Marie or I must be on the premises."

The sergeant said darkly, "It is more likely he was someone wanted by the police, who thought an empty house in a lonely place would be a fine place to hide."

"But he knew about Oliver Abercrombie," Johnny objected. "Anyway, why should he have designs on Sarah—unless, of course, he thought she might be able to tell him about the treasure?"

"I assure you, there was no treasure," Martin declaimed. "The money came each month from a lawyer in Marseilles. Each month, so long as she was able, Miss Abercrombie would drive with me into St. Crécy where she would cash the check. After her death the checks ceased coming."

"You weren't afraid to leave Marie here alone while you went to St. Crécy?"

Martin laughed abruptly. "Oh, Marie is a lioness. Besides, there was the gun."

"The gun?" Louis sounded bemused. "This is the first we have heard of a gun."

"It belonged to the old man. Perhaps the son brought it back from the First War. How should I know? It was before our time. Old Madame said it had never been fired, and by that time no doubt it was too fouled to be of any use. She showed it to us one day and asked if I knew how to fire it. 'People have a right to defend their own property,' she said."

"Had she a license?" demanded the sergeant. "And where is it now?"

"She made me drive her out one day and throw it into a rubbish dump in the woods. Perhaps her voices told her."

"Voices?"

"Oh, she was crazy during that last year or two, would stumble up and down, talking to herself—or shadows—ghosts for all I know. Or of course she might have been afraid someone would break in and find the gun and threaten her with it. Even if it couldn't be fired it was still a lethal weapon. Marie was against it—throwing it away, I mean. She said it gave her a feeling of security to have it in the house, even if it was useless."

"If she was really as crazy as a coot she may have had a persecution mania," offered Johnny, "and started suspecting everyone, even you. I had an aunt . . ."

"We are not concerned with your aunt, monsieur," said the sergeant. "The young English girl has disappeared and we do not think it was of her own free will. Her handbag and passport have been found, she was expecting a visitor . . ."

"Oliver?" exclaimed Martin.

"Me," said Johnny succinctly.

"Madame warned her not to stay here alone," reflected

Martin, "but the English always know best. If she had agreed to go then, I could be with my wife and her daughter at this moment."

"When did Madame meet the young lady?" the curé intervened.

"It was Tuesday evening, we were just leaving the villa, I had to drive Madame into Pau . . ."

The curé shook his head. "No, Martin, you forget. You drove Madame into Pau on Tuesday morning, Marie also. I met you later in the village."

"Is that so?" demanded the sergeant. "Then who was the woman Miss Hollis met that night?"

Martin looked like a man standing against a wall waiting for the rattle of guns.

"It was Madame," he said at last. He turned to the curé. "It's true what I said. I did drive her and Marie into Pau, but—she came back after Marie's train had departed." He glared around at them all, like a wild animal that finds itself unexpectedly in a net. "We did not expect the girl till the next day, there was no harm—Madame sent a telegram to the hotel at Biarritz—I was to drive her in the following morning. No one would have been the wiser if this girl had not come before she was expected. Anyway, Madame was out of the villa on Tuesday night; she can know nothing of Miss Hollis's disappearance."

"We're wasting time with all this talk," protested Johnny. "The first thing to be done is to find this Abercrombie chap and see what sort of alibi he has."

The curé put a hand on his arm. "It is not for us, my son, to tell the police how to conduct their affairs."

"If you want volunteers," Johnny continued eagerly, paying no heed, but the sergeant said, "Thank you, monsieur, we have our own methods of dealing with these matters. We have your address? Then, if there is nothing more you can tell us . . ."

"But where the hell do you start?" cried Johnny.

"You also may return to your wife whenever you please,"

the sergeant continued, turning to Martin. "We may need you again, if fresh evidence turns up. Rest assured that we shall do everything possible. A pity there is no photograph." He sighed. "Still, we can circulate a description . . ."

"How about calling in the British Consul?" asked Johnny hazily. "Or even the C.I.D.? Criminal Investigation Department, Scotland Yard to you," he added.

"Monsieur Bryce," said Louis, scarcely troubling to conceal his exasperation, "I must request you to accept my word that at this stage there is nothing you can do."

"That's what you think," muttered Johnny. Like Crook, whom he had yet to meet, he might have said he wasn't going to be dictated to by a lot of frogs. He had another card literally up his sleeve, and he reckoned the time had come for him to play it.

8

Mr. Crook was moving happily around his room at the Hotel Collioure, slamming his few possessions into a case of about the same vintage as the curé's bicycle, when he got a message that he was wanted on the telephone. In this rather primitive hotel, guests had to come down to the hall to take their calls, so down he bounced to hear a young man, whose voice was completely unknown to him, saying urgently, "Mr. Crook? Mr. Arthur Crook? The lawyer?"

"I never heard there were two of us. Who's that?"

"You won't know my name"—even over the wire the speaker's youth was evident—"but you'll remember Sarah Hollis."

And of course Crook did.

"Sugar at the gates of doom?"

"The Villa Abercrombie."

"That's what I said. Well, she wouldn't be told. The House of Usher, I warned her, and we all know what happened there. What is it this time?"

"She's vanished."

"Gone back bag and baggage to her native land," suggested Crook buoyantly. "Just what I'm proposing to do myself."

"But you can't. And she hasn't. You gave her your card, so you must have been prepared to give her help if she needed it, and she needs it all right, and by this time she must know it."

"You realize I ain't a policeman?"

"Thank goodness for that. The place is crawling with them."

"Looking for the body?"

There was a moment's silence. Then the voice said, "That's not very funny."

Mr. Crook recovered himself. "I said body, not corp," he pointed out. "Where do you imagine I come in?"

"You gave her your address in Bordeaux. You must have had a premonition. Besides, there's no one else."

"Not you?"

"I don't rate much."

"No family?"

"She never spoke of one. She lives with two girls near the zoo."

"Very convenient for anyone who wants her out of the way. Any suggestions as to why anyone should?"

"Not exactly. There was a mysterious stranger calling at the villa, though—risen from the dead, she told me."

"That's more like," approved Crook.

"And there was this malpractice on the car." He explained.

"Are you connecting the one with the other?"

"It wouldn't surprise me. I don't think she was ever meant to get back to the villa in one piece."

"Having seen the car she was travelin' in, I'm surprised she turned up in one piece in the first place," said Crook candidly. All the same, I don't know how I can butt in. Like I said, I ain't the police, just a yellow dog of a lawyer. Why, I don't even have a work permit."

"Don't tell me you're in France for a holiday."

"What's that?" inquired Crook genially. "No, I'm on the job, but—where are you speaking from?"

"St. Crécy. I've been working at St. Mariole at a garage there, but Monsieur Binet gave me the sack this morning; he doesn't care for police buzzing round asking inconvenient questions."

"You can't blame him. Bluebottles ain't to everyone's taste. All the same . . ."

"So I moved into St. Crécy. I thought a little privacy might be desirable. My landlady doesn't care about the police either. Well, if you won't represent Sarah, how about taking me on? It looks as though I'm going to need some help."

"Not giving me a confession?" hazarded Mr. Cautious Crook.

"I don't know where Sarah is, if that's what you mean, and so far I haven't knocked off the sergeant, though that may be merely a matter of time. But they've got their eye on me. I can't cross the street without this flatfoot blundering after me. I can see him from where I'm standing, wanting to make sure I shan't blow up the telephone, I suppose."

"Why didn't you say all this before?" demanded Crook. "Trouble with my profession is it's usually easier if you have a client you can put your finger on." Frivolity fell from him like a cloud from the sun; the very air seemed brighter.

"How soon can you be here?" Johnny urged. No idiotic questions about costs or fees, Crook noted with approval. He liked that. People should put their personal enthusiasms first, not just measure them by pounds, shillings and pence—or possibly in this case by francs and centimes. Anyway, he was a lineal descendant of Robin Hood, his rich paid for his poor, and it all worked out fine. Arthur Crook contrived to make a bit of a living, too.

"How far?" he asked.

"Say 250 kilometers, possibly a bit less."

"What's that in Queen's English?"

"Roughly 150 miles."

"Where's the rendezvous? Better make it a bar. One thing about these French pubs is you can linger as long as you like without going bankrupt."

"There's a place—I'm speaking from it now—called Le Chat Qui Rit—they're dead nuts on cats round here—"

"Hang around then. If they should beat me to it—the gendarmes, I mean—though I don't know why they should unless you're holding out on me—leave a message with Monsieur le proprietaire."

He hauled out his auto club map as soon as he had rung off and got back to his room. Must have thought I was a mouse when I registered, he reflected. He had to go backward more or less to get out of the room. He knew most of the short cuts in his own country, but foreign lands were different. When he had mapped out his route he snapped the locks of his bag, carried it down himself, paid his bill, said a hearty *au revoir* to the expectant hands waiting by the door—he'd paid for service, hadn't he, and what he'd had wouldn't cover a prewar threepenny piece—and off he went.

The sun was out this morning and he felt all the exhilaration of the chase. He didn't blame foxhunters, only felt sorry for them that they couldn't find anything nearer their own size than poor bloody Reynard. It didn't occur to him until he had covered quite a distance that he had not asked for his client's name. Still, nothing to worry about. It never occurred to him he wouldn't be recognized the instant he set foot inside the bar, but if by any chance he wasn't he was perfectly capable of announcing himself in a voice a town crier might envy.

When he arrived at Le Chat Qui Rit he picked out Johnny at once. For one thing, he was the only Englishman there, and Crook had an unerring nose for his own countrymen.

"What's the beer like?" he inquired conversationally, pulling out a chair and dropping his brown bowler on the tabletop.

"I haven't sampled it. This stuff isn't bad." Johnny was drinking wine.

Mr. Crook shook his head. "Can't teach an old dog new tricks. By the way, what's the moniker, or is that another mystery?"

"Mon—? Oh, I see. Bryce, Johnny Bryce. Job—seeing the world. Since I came down from college, that is."

"Been over long?"

"Six months in France. I like it. And I'm in no hurry to join the ratrace."

"Don't let 'em fool you," advised Crook ordering beer. "Rats a different color, talking a different language, that's the only difference. Now—I've come a long way to hear this—how do you imagine I can help Sugar?"

"Isn't that your problem? I'll tell you all I know." He outlined the case as far as he could see it. "I'll tell you this, though; she wasn't alarmed by this fellow, the one calling himself Oliver Abercrombie. According to the evidence, the real one's dead."

"So why should he object to another fellow using his name when it was no longer any good to him?" Crook glanced around and the barman hurried up with the beer.

"The chap to talk to," Johnny persisted, "is the local curé. He's a queer bird but he knows what he's talking about."

"Point is, will he talk back to me? These are his people, remember—noblesse oblige and all that."

"He seems to accept a responsibility for Sarah, if only because she was resident in his parish. It was he who got the police interested; they wouldn't have listened to me."

"Fact is, I've been warned off. Enough to make you think they're in league with the criminals."

"You're on," said Crook simply. "Mind you, we shall look a prize pair of fools if this turns out to be another case of a lady having second thoughts."

"Oh, it won't be that," Johnny assured him. "Even a girl like Sarah must know you can't get far without your passport. What I don't dig is why anyone should suppose she could be a danger to him," he wound up.

"You have to hand it to her, she's a fast worker," said

Crook admiringly. "Arrived in *la belle France* Monday night and—what is it today? Friday?—she's got the local police, the local Church, and the local British resident by the heels—to say nothing of X. By the way, any chance of getting in touch with Madame?"

"I think she's on a yacht."

"We ain't living in the Ice Age," Crook pointed out. "There's something called wireless. Be a help if she'd mentioned the name of the yacht. Still, that's the police's pigeon; we don't want to tread on too many French toes. Now, try and get this into your head. If Sugar's safe as of now, there's no reason she shouldn't be equally safe this time tomorrow, unless somebody blunders. In cases like this the kidnapper usually acts right away or holds out to see which way the cat's going to jump. And don't forget, X is just as likely to try and plug us as the uniformed branch, if we seem to be getting in the way."

"Of course we shall get in the way," said Johnny hotly.

"Softly softly catchee monkey," Crook reminded him. "What's this chap Martin like? Likely to be helpful?"

"He's a wolf," said Johnny in his bluntest voice. "Mrs. Abercrombie must be crazy to suggest he should protect Sarah. As a matter of fact, there's some funny business going on between him and Mrs. A. Sarah interrupted a rendezvous . . ."

"Very tactless," agreed Crook, "but he'd hardly knock her on the head for that. Anyway, their private affairs ain't our business; the only person we're interested in is Sugar. Where's Martin now," he added, "or don't you know?"

"The police told him he was free to rejoin his wife."

"Hope he takes his visor with him. When it comes to unreasonableness, a wife has the whole world beat."

"You mean, when she knows about Mrs. Abercrombie? Will that come out?"

"Who knows about it? The curé, you, me, the sergeant, the cops in attendance—you can't really believe no one's going to utter. Even the police are human when they're out of uniform."

"He gets around, doesn't he?" murmured Johnny. "From what I hear, he's got a ladylove not far from the villa. Of course," he added like a man inspired, "he could be playing Mrs. Abercrombie along in the hope of finding out something . . ."

"About the treasure? Have you swallowed that yarn, too? All the same," he added shrewdly, "you could have something there. He don't sound the type to be above a bit of blackmail —our trouble is we don't know much about any of them to date. It's like going to the cinema and coming in in the middle of the big picture. You don't know what happened in Act One; why, there could even be some characters you've never heard of lurking in the wings. I wonder if Martin did go back to Lourdes," he added casually. "It might be worth finding out."

He refused Johnny's offer to accompany him. "I don't want your shadow following me wherever I go," he explained. "And it seems obvious they're going to keep a paternal eye on you pro tem."

"They're wasting their time," said Johnny. "I'm not in any danger."

"They might not agree."

Johnny's face changed. He looked shocked and incredulous. "You're not suggesting they might think *I* know more of this business than I'm telling?"

"Who knows what a frog thinks? Still, most likely they're only giving you protection. And don't tell me you don't need it. You could be a key witness, and they're just the kind the opposition likes to see at the bottom of the deep blue sea. Keep your eyes peeled and your ears on sticks," he added. "I'll be in touch."

After Johnny had taken his reluctant departure Crook went inside to make his own arrangements with the proprietor. The accommodation offered him wouldn't have satisfied the standards of the British Travel Association, but they say we all have to eat a peck of dirt before we die, and Crook had the stomach of a camel. Anyway, the sound of voices under the window, the clink of bottles, the general argy-bargy, were music to his ears. It reminded him he was still in a world of living men.

At Lourdes, which he reached in the middle of the golden afternoon, he found most of the shops closed. He found the pastry cook without much difficulty. Behind the counter a big fat man moved lightly to and fro, stretching up easily to reach long, powdery loaves, bread studded with seeds and shaped like a hoop. Auguste, reflected Mr. Crook. Well, he would be kept busy for a while. And, after all, it was Marie he had come to see. A few men in working clothes sitting just opposite at Le Petit Cheval looked with interest at the big yellow car. Crook didn't mind; the time might well come when it would be an advantage to be remembered.

Off he went to the back of the shop; it was obvious that the pastry cook lived above his business premises; there were nice white curtains, a flowerpot on the window sill. The door was opened by a short, determined-looking woman, who looked like a couple of Auguste's own plump currant buns; she had snapping black eyes, good teeth and a faint black mustache. That one wasn't married for her beauty, decided Crook, and he felt a sneaking sympathy for Martin. Though, as he would have told you, he was not one for the ladies himself, he could think of more attractive bedfellows.

"Madame Ribaud?" He flashed out one of his immense, ridiculous cards and shoved it into her unwilling hand. "Wonder if I could have a word with your husband."

"He is not at home." Marie started to close the door, but he stuck his big foot across the step.

"Any notion where I might find him?"

"He has his work, monsieur."

"Meaning the Villa Abercrombie. Ah, but that's locked and the police are in possession."

"The police?" Up came her little sallow face, full of apprehension. "Why should the police be there?"

Crook glanced over his shoulder, up and down the narrow street. Heads had appeared at a number of windows, two women brought out wooden chairs and set them on the sizzling pavement. In so quiet a world Crook supposed that even an unusual fly crossing the windowpane would attract attention.

"Nice neighbors you've got," he offered.

Marie hesitated an instant, then reluctantly invited him to come in. The small, square hall was full of darkness; he blinked after the brilliance of the light outside. Then she brought him into a room that compelled his open admiration.

"*La chambre de ma tante,*" he said reverently, his bulging glance moving from the ball-fringed tablecloth to the overmantel with its red plush shelves and innumerable ornaments and photographs, a number of the last framed in crepe. "My mother used to have a room like this," he confided. "Cozy." That reminded him of Sarah again. 'You make things cozy,' she had said. He wondered how cozy they were for her at this moment.

Marie did not even pretend any interest in the late Mrs. Crook's parlor. She did not even offer him any hospitality.

"What is this about police at the villa, monsieur?"

"On account of the English girl. You knew one was expected."

Impatiently Marie gestured toward an overstuffed little chair onto which he rather fearfuly lowered his weight.

"I know that she arrived," she said.

"So you have seen Martin?" exclaimed Crook.

"I know, because I spoke to her from the bistro. I wished to know if my husband was still at the villa."

"When would this be?" asked Crook.

She thought for a moment, then decided it would have been on Thursday.

"That's the night she vanished."

"I know nothing of that, monsieur. She told me my husband was not there, she was expecting him on account of a strange man who had called . . ."

"That 'ud be Oliver. Seems Madame didn't trust him and thought she should have some protection."

Marie uttered a sound not quite a laugh, more like a sneer. She don't seem to think too well of Martin in the role of guardian angel, he reflected. And it could be, of course, she was right.

"Madame seems to have been very concerned about her," he offered. "Took a shine to her that first night perhaps. They met at the villa," he added.

Marie shook her head. She had thin black hair pulled back from a lined forehead; her face shone as though it had been polished along with her son-in-law's buns.

"No, monsieur. Miss Hollis did not meet Madame."

"I'm afraid she did, you know. This may be a bit of a shock to you, but we had it from Martin's own lips."

"Madame left Pau for Biarritz on Tuesday morning. My husband drove us in, he bought our tickets, hers for Biarritz, mine to come here. I tell you, monsieur, I saw her sitting in the window of the carriage wearing that foolish pink hat. Such hats," she added venomously, "may be the mode in Paris, here they are absurd."

"Well, yes," Crook agreed, beginning to feel a bit hot under the collar, and hoping she wouldn't make a dead set at him when he told her the facts, "but after your train had gone Madame changed her mind and went back to the villa with Martin."

He had anticipated ferocity, incredulity, rage, but Marie displayed none of these things.

"Is that what my husband told you?" Her voice sharpened and thinned. "You have seen Martin?"

"He turned up at the villa last night in obedience to orders. Only he was a bit too late; the bird had already flown. Mind you, he didn't want to tell us about Madame, but Sugar—Miss Hollis—had mentioned the meeting to the curé and a young chap she'd met there, so Martin had to come clean. Sugar wasn't expected till the next day . . ." His voice trailed off unconvincingly.

"What Martin says cannot be true, monsieur. I myself saw Madame depart."

"Well," hazarded Crook a bit stupidly, "perhaps she returned on a later train. No?" For Marie was again shaking her head.

"The person Miss Hollis met at the villa that night was not Madame. Only a stranger would consider it for a moment. You did not meet her, monsieur." It was a statement, not a question.

"Not yet had the pleasure," Crook mumbled.

"To Madame, Martin was the man who drove her to and fro, weeded her garden; she inherited him with the furniture and the old black car. He was no more to her than that. Already she had spoken of selling the villa. It had been our home for twenty years, but did she think of that? Or of what might happen to us? I tell you, monsieur, to her Martin was not a man at all."

"If you say so," said Crook. "Then who was the lady?"

"Of course"—Marie seemed to be speaking half to herself—"he did not expect the young girl that night. None of us did. The telegram she sent was delayed. Armande, the one who brings the milk and messages must have forgotten. Madame came down to the lodge carrying it in her hand. 'Miss Hollis has decided to come a week earlier than arranged,' she said. 'Someone must be here to meet her. I shall be with my friends, so you must decide between you which of you will remain.' My poor Celline was crying for her *maman*, so it was agreed that Martin should return when he had taken us to Pau and make preparations. Then, after her arrival, he should join us here."

"And he didn't come—and you started wondering—and you rang the villa. How did Sugar sound?"

"She told me that Madame was sending Martin back."

"How was she going to get hold of him?" inquired Crook. "You don't have a telephone. Or did she get through here?"

Marie put her hand to her head, as if all these questions bewildered her, as well they might.

"That I had not considered. Only, monsieur, I tell you this. Miss Hollis did not meet Madame, because Madame was at Biarritz."

"Meaning you could put a name to the lady she did meet?"

Marie nodded.

According to local gossip Martin has a nice bit of crumpet tucked away somewhere, Johnny had told him. And, of course, Marie had known, hadn't perhaps been particularly surprised. All the same, a charging bull would hardly be more dangerous than Marie now. The risks these husbands take, Crook reflected, thanking his stars once again for his own single blessedness. "You think," he said delicately, wishing he'd brought a suit of chain mail along, "he may be holed up with her now?"

"How can I say, monsieur? You tell me he is not at the villa, I tell you he is not here . . ."

"Stalemate," Crook agreed. "All the same, what was the idea telling Sugar the lady was Madame?"

Marie shrugged. "Who can say? Perhaps he did not tell her, perhaps she supposed her to be Madame Abercrombie, and Martin . . ."

"Let it go by default?"

"Why not? She and Madame would never meet, the girl would return to England first, how would Martin know she had spoken to the curé—ah yes, she told me that when I telephoned—it would seem a harmless deception."

"'What a tangled web we weave . . .'" murmured Crook. "Well, the ball's come back and bounced well and truly on his own head now, hasn't it? You couldn't suggest any address where I could find your husband?"

Marie's pale face swelled and darkened; hurriedly he withdrew the question. "If he should turn up give me a buzz," he pleaded. "Here's the number." He gave her the telephone number of The Laughing Cat. Not that he anticipated Martin would surface in Lourdes. Not if he knew his onions. Me, reflected Mr. Crook, I'd as soon face a lady cobra, hood puffed, fangs flickering, the lot.

There was a note waiting for him from Johnny when he got back. It said that he had found the name of Oliver's hotel, only the chap had pulled out, leaving no address. "Still,"

Johnny wrote, "that car of his, an olive-green Panther, is going to be pretty conspicuous." Johnny had also discovered the name of Martin's inamorata, one Madame Françoise Auberon, said to be a widow, living in a cottage called Les Hirondelles that, like the villa, seemed to be in the middle of nowhere.

Crook rang up Johnny at the immensely superior hotel where he was staying—superior to The Laughing Cat, that is. "I do like a chap who doesn't let the grass grow under his feet," he approved. "I'll tell you one thing, Johnny, this is going to be a very weird business. No, I don't know where Sugar is right now, any more than I know where Madame is. It could be she really is in Biarritz. Martin didn't go home last night by the way. If you should happen to run across him you might ask what arrangements Madame made for having her letters forwarded—if any. I'm going into Pau tomorrow and I'm relying on you to keep those flatfoot shadows off my trail. I'm warning you just in case anything should happen and I don't get back on time, though I'd die of shame," confessed Crook—"assuming I wasn't dead already"—if I thought a frog could do me in, when I think of all the true-blue Britishers who've tried and failed. Still, we have to put Sugar's interest first, don't we? Tell you what, you come along and eat with me tomorrow night, and it could be I'll have something to report."

He wouldn't say any more. He didn't think it likely anyone was tapping the telephone, but there are some chances even chaps like Arthur Crook don't take. Next morning bright and early he departed for Pau.

9

At Pau he went straight to the station. There was a chance, though a slender one, that he might discover someone who remembered the outrageous pink hat. He played it up for all he was worth—*chapeau de rose avec les fleurs bouffantes*—with a wealth of gesture that would have arrested the attention of a stone image. "*Un homme,*" he continued carefully, "*que a acheté deux billets, un pour Biarritz au première, un autre pour Lourdes deuxième.*" He attracted the same sort of curiosity as a two-headed pig would have done. A porter lounging near came a bit closer, and that was Crook's first piece of real good luck, because this man recalled a lady with a remarkable pink hat who had refused his services on the ground that she was already provided for.

The conversation that followed was a tribute to everyone concerned when it is remembered that Crook's French had never progressed beyond Standard One—and he had forgotten some of that—while the porter and the ticket clerk were equally ignorant of English. Crook's gestures were magnificent. He asked first about the lady. *"Grande? Petite? Belle? Et les bagages?"* Part of his trouble was he wasn't quite sure what he was being told. What he did gather was that the lady was not tall, not a beauty though her clothes were elegant, and her luggage seemed to consist of a single black case—the porter indicated the size.

She must have had other boxes, Crook told himself. Going for a cruise. Assuming that that's what she really had in mind.

Point is, he told himself, which is the bigger liar, Marie or her husband? Could be they broke about even.

Because within a few minutes it became obvious that Marie also was deceiving him. She couldn't have seen Madame leaving the station, because the train she must have caught left the station five minutes before the one for Biarritz. Another odd point was that Madame had apparently chosen a local train, though it would have been easy to go by the express, with a restaurant car attached. Ergo, Madame never meant to reach Biarritz.

"You're dead sure the passenger in the pink hat actually traveled in the train?" he demanded impressively of the porter. "I don't mind paying for information and my rates are as high as anyone's, but I want facts, not fairy tales. Could it be the lady changed her mind at the last minute?" The porter, however, stuck like glue to his original story. It must have been some hat, Crook thought, but already he was beginning to suspect the hat itself had been part of the plot. He asked about Marie, but Marie, that little hen sparrow, had attracted no attention at all.

He began to wonder if it might be necessary to go to Biarritz. If so, Johnny could do that chore—probably enjoy it. He asked the porter the way to the post office. Johnny had said something about a telegram that Mrs. Abercrombie was presumed to have sent; or rather, a telegram that Martin declared Mrs. Abercrombie had sent, which might prove quite a different thing.

At the post office he discovered to his chagrin that the gestures and careful phrases that had served him well enough at the station were of little service to him here. He found himself confronted by a blank stupidity he hadn't expected to find outside his own country. Still, post offices, like wolves, were probably the same wherever you found them.

"*Pneumatique*," he urged the assistant behind the counter, and was presented with a form. Instead of displaying gratitude he shook his head and shoved it back. He yearned for the good old days when English was a universal tongue; for himself, he couldn't think why anyone should want anything different. Someone swept him unceremoniously away from his place and started to jabber French like a machine gun. Crook waited till the interloper was through and started again, with no more success than before. A tall man with eyes of a markedly deep blue, who had been watching from the farther end of the post office, reflected that a trier like that might be there all day, so he moved up casually to say in a courteous voice, "Can I be of any help?"

Crook turned, his huge face abeam. "Spika da lingo? Look, I'm trying to trace a telegram dispatched on Tuesday last, sometime during the morning, sent to Biarritz. No, I don't know the address; that's what I'm hoping to learn from the telegram when I see it. I suppose they do keep copies in France?" he added gloomily.

"If you don't know the address, do you know who it was sent to?"

"Some hotel, I fancy. I know the signature though. Abercrombie."

The tall man's dark brows lifted. "You must have some reason . . ."

"Sure I've got a reason. Look, you tell this tailor's dummy I'm trying to trace a telegram that I'm assured was sent but was never received. Go on, you can't let the frogs put one over on you."

"I'd have said it was the other way round," the stranger murmured, but he turned to the clerk and entered into a sharp exchange of views with him. How he did it Crook couldn't have told you, but within a minute or so he was being presented with the copy of a telegram that had been sent to Biarritz on the previous Tuesday and signed Abercrombie.

"What you wanted?" he asked politely, handing it to Crook. The telegram canceled a room in the name of Abercrombie booked for that night, which was precisely what Crook had anticipated.

"Just how Mother makes it," he agreed in exuberant tones. "Here, what's the damage? Don't tell me you get anything for free this side of the Channel. . . . Well, of course there had to be a telegram to stop the talk."

If the stranger was surprised at being taken, even so vaguely, into Crook's confidence, he didn't display it. They found a pleasant-looking pub, and Crook invited his benefactor to have one on him.

"Couldn't have got this without you," he agreed generously.

It was very pleasant basking in the sun. Crook's anxieties seemed suddenly to have fallen from him; he became positively loquacious. The stranger listened, made an occasional comment, and let Crook keep on talking. After a second round the lawyer lumbered to his feet. "Time and tide," he quoted. Clichés were his meat and drink. "Be seeing you, if we're lucky."

He got into the Superb, and off he went, as busy as a bee. The tall man watched him out of sight.

"Lucky being the operative word," he said aloud.

If Crook had stopped a minute or two longer he would have seen this chance acquaintance drive off in his own car, as showy in its own way as the Superb. It was a Panther, olive-green in color, and Sarah would have recognized it at once. It had passed her on the road from the lake on her first momentous day at the villa.

The presbytery at St. Mariole was Crook's next port of call. The proposal he was going to make was so outrageous that only an inspired simpleton, such as he understood the curé to be, would have considered it. The curé was out visiting. Crook and Eugénie stood jabbering at one another for a minute before she got her message home. Monsieur le Curé was out, he was busy, would be busy on his return; in short, he had had enough of *les anglais*. Crook found himself staring at the outside of the door. Philosophically he returned to the Superb and set himself to wait. It was possible to hear the creaking of the ancient bone-shaker bicycle before the rider came into view, and when he did it was to find Crook on his feet by the front door. Crook remembered Johnny telling him the curé spoke English, though possibly by this time the old boy was beginning to find Anglo-French relations starting to fray a bit. Still, Crook played the only two cards he had, Sarah Hollis and Johnny Bryce. The curé got a garbled idea that Crook was in some way connected with Scotland Yard—the Yard would have died of chagrin to know this, but no one was going to tell them. Eugénie's look as they came together into the house was sheer death, but Crook's experience and the curé's profession made them indifferent to that kind of thing.

"You bring news of Mademoiselle?" the curé suggested. He lit a pipe that looked as if it might have come out of a Hans Andersen fairy tale.

"I don't know where she is, if that's what you mean, though I could make a guess. What's worrying me just as much at the present time is the whereabouts of Madame Abercrombie. You see, if I win my guess, the lady never left the villa at all."

The curé called for coffee and cognac. Marie answered the call with suspicious celerity. "She don't understand English, I take it?" Crook inquired.

"Quelques petits mots," the curé reassured him.

"Must be tantalizing. Here you are with a crime right on your doorstep and it's mostly Greek to her." It occurred to him a bit late in the day that perhaps the curé didn't share his burning interest in crime. The coffee and cognac arrived, the coffee bitter as Marah by Earl's Court tastes; if brandy wasn't Crook's normal tipple, at least it was better than the coffee.

"There used to be a song when I was a boy," Crook said. 'It's the little things that matter, don't you see?' It's the little things that are bothering me here—the little lies that don't make sense if my hunch is right. For instance, why should Marie say she saw Madame leave the station at Pau when it can't conceivably be true? Marie's train went first."

"She means perhaps that she saw Madame in the train," suggested the curé charitably.

"That ain't what she said. And then—here's a bigger whopper for you—Martin told you he'd driven both ladies in that morning."

"That is so." The curé considered. "I met him in the village."

"Coming home? I see. And when you heard his story about Madame returning to the villa after all, you didn't smell a rat?"

The curé sipped his cognac. "You think I should have known what he said was untrue?"

"You met him coming back from Pau," Crook insisted.

The curé laid down his pipe. "Yes, that is what I did."

"And he had the car? So—wouldn't you expect to see Madame somewhere around, *if she had come back*?"

"I had no reason to disbelieve him. Madame had let everyone know about her trip."

"Sure, sure," agreed Crook. "But weren't you there when he explained how Sugar came to meet the lady?"

"I think I understand," the curé agreed after a moment. "It should have occurred to me. Martin was alone when I met him in St. Mariole. And no one in the village had seen Madame return—oh, it would be difficult to conceal that one."

"I knew you'd get my point." Crook beamed. He could see the curé was, like himself, able to believe six impossible things before breakfast, but no nitwit for all that.

"So Madame did *not* return," the curé finessed.

"My point being that she never left. Well, think, what did anyone see—what did the railway porter see? A dame in a pink hat sitting at a train window—a slow train, mark you—

and starting off. He's dead sure of that. What he *didn't* see was Marie following her husband to the reservation office to collect her ticket. And another thing he didn't see was the sort of luggage you'd expect a lady like Mrs. A. to have with her if she was going on a voyage with a lot of posh friends."

"Monsieur Crook," said the curé, folding his big hands on his knee, "I am a simple parish priest. As a boy I was known as the fool of the family. One does not change as one grows older; one simply develops. Will you please tell me in simple language what you have in mind?"

"Who's kidding who?" murmured Crook. "The point I'm making is that no one can swear he saw Madame on that train—no disinterested party, that is. What they did see was a lady in an extravagant hat, moving off. That's the point, Monsieur le Curé. *They saw a hat.* The same with anyone who may have seen the car driving into Pau. They saw Martin and a passenger wearing a pink hat—from Paris. No one but Madame would own such a hat—ergo, Madame was Martin's passenger. No one saw a lady in a pink hat coming back, no one's seen the pink hat since; the room she'd reserved in Biarritz was canceled. It wouldn't surprise me to know that the party in Biarritz whom Madame was planning to meet had had a call explaining that Madame had had to change her plans. Only seeing we don't know said party's name, and to date no one's suggested Madame may have disappeared, we can't check up on that yet."

"You imply, monsieur, that only one woman left the villa with Martin on Tuesday morning?"

"No one ever saw him with two. I daresay if they was to check they'd find Madame's ticket was never handed in at Biarritz."

"Because she did not arrive?"

"Because she never set out. Listen! Marie puts on the pink hat and sits in the train window where she's bound to be noticed—at least where the hat's bound to be noticed. Surprising really she didn't add a couple of hummingbirds or something. Still, it seems to have attracted attention enough.

Next station she alights and makes her way back to Lourdes. Police might find it instructive to know just what time she arrived, but I daresay she'd have some story ready for them. All she has to do is go into a Ladies—unless she could find an empty railway carriage—pack the hat in the black case and get rid of it somewhere a bit later, change coats, and there she is—Marie Ribaud going to join her daughter who's expecting a baby."

"A very ingenious theory," agreed the curé. "You do not tell me why all this romance is necessary."

"I thought we might get the answer to that at the villa. Now, I daresay the police would sooner let a camel through the eye of a needle than pass me through, but if you was to ask them—well, Sugar *is* one of our nationals and she did come here under Her Britannic Majesty's protection. And you might ask yourself why Martin was so anxious for the girl to believe she'd met Mrs. A. in the flesh. Kind of an alibi," he added, hoping the curé wouldn't probe too far.

Sergeant Louis Grasse was livid when he heard his brother was outside with yet another Englishman. "You can tell them that the case of the missing English girl is now in the hands of Inspector Bertin," he said.

Crook beamed like the morning sun. "Well, whaddya know?" he exclaimed. "Me and the Inspector have met before. He was over in London last year, looking for the bank robber Pelissier. You give him one of my cards." He hauled one out of his pocket. At this rate, he reflected, he'd have to have a new lot printed when he got home.

The sergeant puffed like a pouter pigeon but he was no match for Crook. Within a few minutes the four of them—since even Louis Grasse had not the nerve to suggest keeping the curé out of the discussion—were sitting around a table, and Crook was making his points.

"A thing that sticks in my gullet," he acknowledged, "is the way Marie was so dead sure Sugar couldn't have met Mrs. Abercrombie. It is impossible, she said, or something like that. Nothing's impossible to a man—or woman—while he's still breathing. The curé will back me up in that. So, if she knows it's impossible, don't it sound to you as if she knows the reason?"

"There's one thing you've overlooked, Mr. Crook," said the Inspector briskly. "Martin may have allowed the girl to think she was meeting Mrs. Abercrombie because Marie was coming back the following week and Martin wouldn't want it known that he had his mistress at the villa. He has to live with Marie, remember."

"Well, that's another point I was going to make," said Crook. "Has he? Suppose he and the lady were planning a getaway? He didn't go back to his wife, remember."

"None of this explains why he should wish harm to Miss Hollis."

"Well, we won't know the answer to that till we've had our look-see round the villa. But it seems odd to me that Sugar's car should put itself out of action in a way no car ever has before—without human intervention—and then when that doesn't work, this mystery fellow, Oliver Abercrombie or whatever his real name may be, should surface, and within twenty-four hours she's disappeared. Maybe he didn't fancy the idea of her and her friends moseying round the villa."

The curé spoke out of a long silence. "Louis," he said, "you remember the spade and the fork in the garden shed? There was earth on the tines and . . ."

"It was dried earth," the sergeant reminded him. "We agreed they couldn't have been used to dig Mademoiselle's grave."

"It is not Mademoiselle's grave that Mr. Crook and I have in mind."

Bertin stood up. "It sounds a pretty far-fetched story to me, Mr. Crook," he acknowledged, "but outsiders do sometimes come first past the post." He looked at the sergeant. "The villa is still guarded? Then let us go. I can only add, Mr. Crook, I hope this time for once you are wrong."

In one of his peregrinations Crook had seen a print of a theater set for an evil house. Structurally the villa was different, yet the memory flashed instantly into his mind; the blank, narrow door, the empty windows, the tall, conical roof set like a cap of darkness above dereliction. Here at the villa the sun shone, the air was full of the scent of roses, yet the general impression was one of absence of light.

The four men, followed by gendarmes in a police car, came through the gate and past the garage into the garden. Crook showed no interest in the house, but he walked around the garden as if he really knew something about horticulture. The curé watched him with the most intense interest. In the shed the tools and barrow stood untouched since the police's last visit. Crook moved forward; gently he spun the wheel of the barrow upended against the wall. "See that?" he said, and indicated the little withered plant with its two forlorn golden petals that still clung to the wood. "Kind of a buttercup," he offered. "Marsh marigolds we call 'em; grow in marshy places. Now, there's no wild life in this garden. Martin kept it clean, and don't tell me he wheeled the grass cuttings, such as they were, down to the marshland. Why, there's a handsome compost heap—mentally he applauded himself for not calling it a rubbish dump—below the rose beds; you'd expect him to put all the garden refuse there. So—how come there's a marsh marigold stickin' to the wheel of the barrow?"

The Inspector looked at his sergeant. Louis said slowly, "There is marshy ground in the woods beyond the orchard. There is a stream underground . . ."

"Not the only thing underground," commented Crook with a sudden lapse of taste. It occurred to the Inspector that his tough manner concealed a genuine anxiety.

"No doubt," said Louis with as near a sneer as he dared in the presence of his superiors, "Mr. Crook will explain."

"If Mr. Crook's suspicions are correct, it will not be his duty to supply explanations," rapped out the Inspector tartly. "It is possible, of course, that he may be mistaken." His men came through, carrying spades, to receive their instructions.

"You will doubtless wish to remain and see the result of our investigations." Bertin turned politely to his visitor.

"Puts me in my place, don't he?" murmured Crook without rancor, turning to the curé. That gentleman, with his normal appearance of remaining impervious to the shackles of time, had moved toward the blanket of wild roses that a light wind lifted from the wall; a wave of fragrance enveloped them.

"Pretty!" said Crook, trying to sound the correct social note.

But the curé shivered. "They are too innocent," he said. "There is no place for them here."

The digging party was away for a long time. Crook began to get restive. He never had been able to understand this passion for living in the country. All cows and weeds and a lot of birds that should have known better, waking you before dawn—and not a pub for miles. He stole a glance at the curé, but he was like Patience on a monument. Gone into a trance perhaps. Or communing with his Maker. He was a strange-looking chap, but he gave out strength as a fire gives out heat. Wouldn't like him on the other side, Crook reflected, and that was a compliment. There weren't many men who could make him feel that way.

Time passed, the sun shone, the roses fluttered and bowed. At last came the sound of feet; a gendarme hurried past and went into the house without a word. An instant later the two men heard the sound of the telephone being lifted from its hook. It was so still they might have been waiting for the birth of a world. The voice from within the villa ceased; the man came back the way he had come. Still no one spoke, not until Louis himself came slowly toward them through the orchard.

"They have found her," he said. "Now we are awaiting official identification. She has been shot in the back."

Crook left them to it. The murder of Mrs. Abercrombie was no concern of his. What he had to do was find out what had happened to Sarah Hollis. So he beetled off to lay his plan of campaign with his most likely ally.

10

Sarah opened her eyes to find herself in a square cave of darkness illuminated only by a small bulb hanging in one corner of the room. At first she thought she had reached the halfway house between nightmare and sensibility, the stage where a man dreams fearfully, knows he is dreaming and struggles to set himself free. It was like coming up and up through the trough of a wave; sometimes a second wave comes rolling along to submerge the dreamer, and his struggles must be renewed. But after a minute she realized she was no longer struggling, and that what surrounded her was reality itself. Now she brought memory into play. She knew, of course, she was not in the flat near Regent's Park.

But then I wasn't there when all this began, she reflected hazily. I was at the villa—of course, it's coming back to me now—I was waiting for someone. I went out—why did I go out?

As yet panic had not assailed her; she was too busy trying to piece together the bits of the puzzle. Tranquilly she remained where she was, like someone in a hospital bed.

Someone hit me, she thought, and automatically her hands went to her head. No, it was more like being choked. Only in that case, why aren't I dead? She gave momentary consideration to the possibility that this was perhaps that limbo that may be the state after death. Perhaps I'm a spirit—she surprised herself by a weak giggle. Has the spirit hands and feet as I have? She stretched out her arms, flexing and unflexing her fingers. Oh yes, she had hands all right. She discovered she was lying on a bed in a room she had never seen before. At first she wondered if this might be a hospital, but the bareness, the discomfort, the lack of furniture or hospital equipment, made her discard that idea.

She rolled over and stood up. At all events her feet weren't tied; she noticed, though, that her own shoes had vanished, and in their place she was wearing slippers that were too large for her. She walked through the darkness toward the ineffectual little bulb, and saw that the blackness was due to the fact that shutters had been fastened across the window. She seized the metal bar that held them in place, only to realize that this had been padlocked and resisted all her efforts. Now panic entered the scene. Was it possible that this was a room in one of those mental institutions that cater to the dangerous, the unbalanced, the lunatic fringe? She rushed across to the door and found, as she had feared, it was locked on the other side. She began to hammer on the panels and shout. "Let me out! Let me out!"

She listened but could hear nothing. It occurred to her she might be incarcerated in an empty house. It even occurred too that she might still be at the villa, in one of the unexplored attics. She listened but could hear no sound beyond the window. The room boasted no bell, and when she came to examine her wrist she found her watch had been removed. Nor had she any notion how much time had elapsed since the assault in the villa garden.

If this isn't the villa there's no reason why anyone should

ever find me, she reflected, fighting for self-control. If I've been left here to starve . . . That brought her up short. Left here to die? What nonsense! Unless she were to die of fear. Abruptly she stopped shouting and returned to the bed. If that was the plan, how was it she wasn't starving? Or dirty? Or disheveled? There was no looking glass, no shining surface anywhere that might have helped, but she passed her hands over her hair; it felt smooth and glossy. Her hands were clean.

She walked around the walls. What had appeared to be a cupboard proved to be a door leading to a closet, containing primitive bathroom facilities and a handbasin. She turned the tap and water ran, cooling her hands; she stooped and bathed her face. Another thing she noticed was that there was no dust on the few pieces of furniture, so either she had only been here a few hours or she had been kept under drugs that drowned memory. Think as she might she could recall nothing after the hand had closed her mouth—except the face of the man to whom that hand belonged. She put her own over her eyes. It doesn't make sense, she protested. What harm could I have done you?

That memory started her up once more, she ran across to the door and once again started to thump and scream. This time her efforts met with more success. Feet came up the stairs; they seemed to come from a long way off.

So this isn't the villa, reflected Sarah shrewdly. That was on two floors only. Then why . . .?

The feet stopped, a key was put in the lock of the door, which opened. The landing beyond was bathed in light. So it was morning—at all events night had not fallen. It occurred to her she didn't even know if she had left the villa yesterday or had been unconscious—drugged, she wondered?—for longer than that.

"We do not want all that noise," a brisk voice adjured her. The woman spoke English but with a foreign accent. "I have brought some food," she continued, setting a tray on the table.

"I don't want any food," said Sarah. "I want to know where I am."

"You are in my care."

"But why? I mean, I'm perfectly capable of looking after myself."

"Yes, mademoiselle. Eat your food before it gets cold."

"Whose house is this?"

"Mine, mademoiselle."

"But why should I be in your house?" She saw that the woman had laid a small flashlight on the table and now she snatched it up, casting the beam in her companion's face. The woman fell back, effectually blocking the doorway.

"What on earth does this mean?" demanded Sarah, too weak with surprise to make any attempt to escape. "I know you. You're Mrs. Abercrombie and we met in the villa on Tuesday night. Have you taken leave of your senses? You must be mad to think you'll get away with this, whatever your motive."

"It is not I who is mad, mademoiselle."

"When my friends realize I'm not at the villa . . ."

"Which are they, mademoiselle?"

"Of course, I have friends interested in my well-being . . ."

"In that case it is surprising they permitted you to travel alone, a girl in your state. But perhaps all this is lies; perhaps you have escaped from somewhere—how do I even know you are whom you claim to be?"

"You've only got to look at my passport. Where's my bag?" Her eyes searched the room.

"You had no bag when you were found, mademoiselle. That is why we supposed you were one of the unfortunates from the mental asylum."

"Why not ring them up and ask them if there's one missing."

"That has been done. And the answer is yes. Someone will be coming for you quite soon."

This is really happening, Sarah told herself. It doesn't seem possible, but it's true. Of course, she knows who I really am, so why—why? She said the word aloud, "Why?" and was shocked to hear her voice emerge as a croak.

"You will be in good hands," the woman assured her soothingly."

"Wouldn't it be more sensible to get in touch with my friends and get one of them to come over and identify me?"

"If you will give us the address—but I understood there was no one."

She thought instantly of Johnny, but wisdom counseled her to lie low where he was concerned. It was like waking in the middle of a nightmare. For some reason she couldn't yet fathom, she was a danger to this woman. But I don't know anything, she protested silently. How could I possibly hurt you?

"I should like my bag and my watch back," she announced. "What time is it anyway?"

"What difference does that make to you? Anyway, it is time to eat."

"You've taken my shoes," Sarah complained. "I can't walk in these."

"You had no shoes."

"I certainly had shoes when I got to the villa. Why—it's beginning to come back to me—I had shoes when I went out driving next day. The car!" she added.

"Car, mademoiselle?"

"My car that suddenly went wrong. Only not quite wrong enough. It was meant to crash altogether, wasn't it?"

"You had no car when you were found, mademoiselle. But perhaps," she added soothingly, "there was once a car that crashed. Perhaps that would account for your condition now. Try and think—what else do you remember?"

"Don't talk to me as if I were a lunatic. I remember everything perfectly. I was at the villa and you were there—and Martin."

The woman shook her head. "You are making a mistake. Whom do you think I am?"

"You're Mrs. Abercrombie, of course. I rented your villa

and I came a week early, and you were there, only you couldn't wait. So Martin said he would come back, but there was an accident . . ."

"Another car accident, mademoiselle?"

"So he rang up to say he wouldn't come, and I said it didn't matter, I should be all right. And then Oliver . . ."

"Eat your food," said the woman gently. "It will only confuse you to try to remember. Martin—Oliver—this Mrs. Abercrombie . . ."

"She said she was Mrs. Abercrombie. *You* said you were Mrs. Abercrombie."

She had a shocking fear that she was going to pass out. "What have you done to me?" she demanded. "Don't think I don't know who he was—I saw his face—that's how I know he was in it with you. You were very clever, only I don't see how I was to know . . ." The room was beginning to spin. "Can't we have some air? The room's suffocating."

"I regret, mademoiselle, I cannot open a window."

"Why not? Are you afraid I should throw myself out? Wouldn't that solve all your problems, though why you should imagine I'm one of them puzzles me. No, do listen, and stop pushing that revolting tray at me—I can't imagine why you had me brought here, unless you're mixing me up with someone else. I mean, I couldn't possibly do you any harm. I don't know anything about you. I never set eyes on you until Tuesday night. I wouldn't even know who you were if you hadn't told me you were Mrs. Abercrombie."

"No, mademoiselle." The woman's calm was unruffled. "I have never told anyone that that was my name."

"But you did. I called you Mrs. Abercrombie." She stopped abruptly. It was as if a light had suddenly been turned on. "Is that why—oh, you're crazy all right. You're not Mrs. Abercrombie."

"I keep telling you."

"But you didn't tell me *that* night. Why? Why?" She leaned forward, her body trembling, her hands clasped. "Where is Mrs. Abercrombie?" she whispered. "What have you done with Mrs. Abercrombie?"

"I regret," said the woman in a voice that sounded as if she meant it. She took something out of her pocket, something small and glittering. It was a hypodermic syringe.

"No, no," whispered Sarah, shrinking back. "Not that. Of course, that's what you used before—when you brought me here, I mean. That's why I don't remember anything, why I feel so queer. I do, you know."

"You will feel better when you have slept. Presently, when you wake up, you will find yourself at home . . ."

"My home is in England, as you know very well. England is where I'm going."

"Yes. Perhaps. When you are well."

She can't really get me shut up, Sarah thought. There must be rules and regulations, doctors' certificates. But, of course, that isn't what she means. I shall just—disappear. Or there'll be another accident to the car, and this time they'll make sure it's fatal. She was instantly convinced that this was the plan they had in mind. A drugged girl in a runaway car—there would never be any proof.

"Where is my car?" she asked, and the woman gave her another pitying glance.

"You will have a car to drive in," she promised. "A very fine car, and this time there will be no accidents."

"I wish I could understand what all this is about," Sarah said. "Of course, I realize now who you are. You and Martin . . ." She saw a flash of anger cross the woman's face. "But that's all I could tell anyone; I'm not a danger to you. Anyway, why should I be interested?"

They were interrupted by the loud pealing of a bell from the street below. The woman put up her head.

"Isn't it the one you're expecting?" Recognizing an element of doubt, Sarah went on tauntingly, "But perhaps you're afraid it's the police?"

"If it is the police they will be here for you, not for me."

"Why should I mind the police coming?" Before she could be prevented Sarah opened her mouth and began to scream.

"Up here," she shouted. "I'm up here."

At the same time she dashed at the woman's rather solid

figure as if she would butt her way through. But she was no match for her enemy. In a moment she felt her arms gripped and twisted behind her, and before she could cry out at the brutality of the gesture the woman had whipped off a scarf that she wore around her throat and had bound Sarah's arms behind her back. Sarah struggled in vain.

"You've had practice, haven't you?" she gasped. "Who else . . . ?" She felt herself flung back on the bed; without her hands she could not steady herself and fell lumpishly. She heard the door slam and the sound of feet on the stairs, as the bell pealed again.

If this is Martin's woman, she thought, Martin would surely have a key. A new hope sprang up in her. In some manner Johnny had started investigations, she had been traced; it would indeed be the police on the other side of the door.

She heard the slam of the front door, then the sound of voices. There seemed to be some kind of argument going on, voices were raised, there was something like a shout hastily cut off. Johnny, she thought, it must be Johnny to account for all the excitement . . . Then everything went quiet for about a minute, and at last feet sounded on the stairs. Not the police, decided Sarah; there was nothing official or military about this ardent step. Not Madame either, she would recognize anywhere that firm, deliberate tread.

"Johnny!" she called. "I'm in here, Johnny."

The door was opened and a voice said, "Too bad to disappoint you; this isn't your lucky day. Who's Johnny when he's at home?"

She struggled up, hampered by her bonds, to find herself staring into the face of the man who called himself Oliver Abercrombie. The puzzle began to fall into place.

"So that's why you turned up at the villa; you were in the plot from the start. Why didn't I guess? It was too much of a coincidence that you should happen to arrive just at the same time as I did. And it was you who meddled with the car, and that's why you wouldn't stop, because . . ."

"You're worse than I am when it comes to not stopping."

He turned his eyes on her, those strange eyes of a slaty blue; they were gleaming but not with humor or kindness; there was a pitiless look about them. "What did you do to Madame for her to tie you up like that?" She didn't answer that.

"I thought, if you were Johnny, she'd be sure to say I wasn't here."

"But why Johnny? Where does he fit in?"

"I suppose it doesn't occur to any of you that I might have friends?"

"You could do worse than think of me as one of them. I meant that," he added, seeing her incredulous scorn. "I tried to warn you at the villa that a girl like you shouldn't be alone there."

"Why have you come?" she demanded, and she saw his dark brows rise.

"Need you ask? To take you away, of course."

"Take me where?"

"Where you'll be safe. Can't you understand that I really have your interests at heart? I can't explain now. Just be patient. You'll see."

"Battened down under hatches in a lunatic asylum?" She could hardly recognize her own voice. A kind of faintness began to steal over her; it might have been wise to take the food when it was brought. But how could she eat anything in this house? It could be drugged, poisoned even.

"Surely they don't treat the mentally afflicted like that, not unless they're really violent. Though, come to that, you look pretty violent yourself," Oliver commented.

"With my arms tied behind me, so that I feel like a bolster?"

"Ah, but if I untied you you'd make a run for it, wouldn't you? Yes, of course you would, and what would happen then?"

"I should be free."

"For how long? No, you'll have to take my word for it, you're better off with me than if you stayed here, for instance."

"You've given me every reason to trust you, haven't you?"

Sarah gibed. She felt icy-cold, and not simply because there was no heat in the room. Fear flooded over her at the realization of her own helplessness; it was like being drenched under a cold spray. For the first time she could understand how prisoners and the condemned begged for mercy. I'd beg myself, if I thought I had a chance, she admitted to herself.

"Come on," said Oliver more roughly. "We've wasted time enough." He caught her by the shoulder and swung her toward the door.

"I might prefer to stay here," she said obstinately. She still cherished a notion that somehow Johnny would discover her in this place, whereas once she was removed he could follow a cold trail forever.

"Perhaps you would." Oliver's voice thickened with impatience. "Only it doesn't happen to suit me."

"What happened to my bag? You can't expect me to go anywhere with you without a bag?"

"You can manage without it now," he said.

"But you will give it me," she insisted.

"I haven't got it. I suppose it's wherever you left it."

Her heart gave a leap of hope. She had left it at the villa, and Johnny had promised to come that night. When he got no reply he would suspect something was wrong, would break in, and find the bag. And in the bag somewhere was Mr. Crook's card. Of course, he mightn't find it, or see the significance of it if he did, but at least it gave her a germ of hope.

Oliver's arm tightened around her shoulders as they came onto the landing; she looked about her eagerly. Two or three other doors, all closed, opened upon it; at the turn of narrow stairs stood an old Breton chest of black wood with acanthus carvings.

"Is that where they keep the drugs?" she demanded.

"That's enough questions for the time being," Oliver warned her grimly. He pressed her head against the fabric of his coat so that she could not even cry out. She tried to say, "You're hurting my ear," but it came out as a sort of guggle-guggle.

Around the bend of the stairs they came and down into the hall. There was no one in view, but the woman must have been within earshot because Oliver called out something about it not being very long now. Then he had opened the front door, and she saw the long gleaming shape of the Panther a few steps up the road. As his grasp insensibly relaxed, Sarah wrested herself free and leaped forward, but she might have saved herself the trouble. He had overtaken her in an instant, caught her up like a bundle of old washing and dumped her into the back seat. He took a rug and swathed it around her till she was like a cocoon.

"Any more trouble from you," he said grimly, "and I'll gag you into the bargain."

"Aren't you afraid people might think it a bit odd for you to be carrying a passenger gagged and bound?"

"They'd probably assume you were the missing patient from the mental place over the hill. Didn't you know there was one? It's in all the papers—said to be violent. If we do meet any cars you'll be well advised to lie still and look as if you were asleep. It's all for your own good . . ."

"Oh sure," agreed Sarah, but there was no spirit in the rejoinder. Nevertheless, she was resolved—in the words of the old history books—to sell her life dearly. If another car should draw alongside she would yell and yell. It might strike an intelligent passer-by as odd that an escapee from a local madhouse should talk English. This consideration helped to calm her nerves as they sped down the road, which looked as empty as though this were the first day of creation.

"Did you ever hear the name Arthur Crook?" she inquired suddenly.

But apparently it was impossible to trick Oliver.

"I know about Crook. What's your interest?"

"I suppose you're going to try and persuade me you're Arthur Crook."

"No, why?" He sounded genuinely surprised. "I'm Oliver Abercrombie."

"I'd no idea ghosts could be so solid."

"Ghosts?"

"Oh, where's the sense in pretending? Oliver Abercrombie's been dead for more than two years."

There was a brief silence. Then he said, "You're very well informed. Not that it really matters . . ."

"I suppose you had to explain your presence at the villa somehow. I daresay it was a shock to you, my being there at all."

"You can say that again," said Oliver. "I felt—what's the word?—flabbergasted. I simply couldn't believe my eyes."

"You'll have to make a better job of the car next time, won't you?"

He said nothing but his face was hard as flint. Sarah was left with the realization that if they should be stopped she wouldn't have an earthly chance. I probably look like something out of Walpurgis Night, she reflected—hair wild, no makeup, mauled about first by one of them and then the other. The man who called himself Oliver, on the contrary, looked smooth, competent, even elegant; he drove a car that would be any man's envy; oh, anyone would take his word against hers. He was probably even furnished with suitable documents to support his story.

Still, on the bare chance that she was going to have an opportunity of putting her case, she began to assemble it in her mind. Flying from the cottage she had noticed the name painted on the gate—Les Hirondelles. Everyone in the village, Johnny said, knew about Martin's love affair; probably most of them could put a name to the woman. That linked up the pair; that was step Number One. But she's only got to swear she never set eyes on me and I'm back where I started, Sarah realized. Yet surely Mr. Crook, clever Mr. Crook with Johnny as his assistant—like Crook, she discounted the police—could trace some affiliation between that pair of rogues and the superrogue now driving her away to nowhere. If the link existed Crook would find it, given the time. Time was of the essence—it wouldn't help her for Crook to discover the truth when she was beyond benefiting from it.

"That woman," she said suddenly, "at the cottage . . ."

"Madame Auberon?" Oliver's voice sounded absorbed, and she realized he also had his problems. "What about her?"

"What does she hope to get out of this?"

"What a lot of questions you ask."

She fell back against the cushions of the car. This was a solitary part of the countryside with wide, flat fields stretching in all directions. Yet surely, sooner or later, they must come to a village. A village implied houses, a church, a shop, a bistro, people moving in and out . . .

"Unless, of course, they're all having their siesta," she murmured. It was absurd to hope that she could identify her surroundings after two days, and in fact she beheld nothing familiar. After a while, however, she detected a steeple, tall and thin as the finger of righteousness piercing the sky, and her heart lifted again. A church implies a village. But Oliver had seen it, too; Oliver was taking no unnecessary chances. Before they reached the outskirts of the village, whichever it might be, the car swung to the left, taking an ascending road that presently became the kind of path never intended for motor traffic. Now trees appeared, the incline became steeper; even the thrifty French peasantry had not been able to sow crops or any rewarding plants on these hills. The path narrowed until branches were whipping against the windows of the car; they went up by a series of hairpin curves, and at each Sarah held her breath wondering how the big car could turn in so limited a space. At one time it seemed as though the back wheels hung over an abyss, but before she could cry out or even bury her lips in the rug to smother such a cry, they had regained their balance. Up and up they climbed. Now, if anyone passed on the road, it was improbable that the car would be visible. A more modest vehicle would have groaned or bleeped or protested in some way, but the Panther ran on as smoothly as if it were on level ground. For a moment Sarah even forgot her terrors, admiring the driver's skill, until she began to consider the reason for this ascent into anonymity. There could be no house, surely, so high above the road. Ah, but he was not looking for a house—just some place where a body could lie undiscovered until identification became impossible. Oh no, she thought, not that.

"What's the matter?" asked Oliver, without turning his head. "Cold? What have you done with your rug?"

"You must have a tremendous lot at stake to take this chance," she burst forth. "I'm a British subject; we don't like it when our nationals disappear overseas . . ."

"I'm not precisely enjoying it myself," Oliver assured her. "And you're right about my having a lot at stake. It's my life, my whole life."

"I suppose my life isn't of any importance," she burst forth.

"At the moment," said Oliver grimly, "I'm concerned with mine."

The pace of the car had slowed a little; Oliver looked expectantly from side to side. Through the trees Sarah caught sight of a wineshop, scarcely more than a mountain hut. There were three or four men, presumably foresters, sitting in the doorway around a blistered green metal table with playing cards and glasses. Oliver drove quickly past, before she could realize this might be the opportunity she was looking for. Then common sense told her it would be a waste of time to appeal to them; most likely they wouldn't even understand her when she spoke in French. The peasantry of these mountainous districts spoke a rough patois, as difficult for aliens to understand as those same aliens would find the dialects of the English rural areas.

Oliver brought the car to a halt. "Wait here a minute," he said, as though she had any choice. "I have to put through a call from the bistro—possibly two calls. I noticed they had a phone. Now don't try and do anything silly while I'm away. Even if you could break out of the car it wouldn't do you any good. Just take a peep through the windows; that should discourage you. And remember, I'll have you under my eye."

He paused to wind the rug even more closely about her. She supposed that if she could get into the front seat she might be able to sound the horn with her chin, which might bring the winebibbers running, but it would also bring Oliver. She looked down the steep sides of the hills. Without the use of her hands she would be a dead dog within five minutes. As it was, she was so stiff she wondered if she would ever have the full use of her arms again. "I'll be black and blue tomorrow," she said aloud; then realized that by tomorrow it probably wouldn't matter if she was all the colors of the rainbow. And even if she could get out, there was nowhere to go. Indeed, it might provide Oliver with the opportunity he required. A car could run down a fugitive in a matter of seconds, and there would be nowhere to fly from the heartless wheels. Oliver's messages must have been pithy and to the point because it seemed no time before he returned. A moment later they were on their way.

"Where now?" demanded Sarah, trying to sound jaunty.

To her surprise a road had been cut at this height, and progress should now be much faster. Which made it all the more odd that after about ten minutes the Panther began to stammer and halt, then slowed, finally stopped, and no encouragement from Oliver could get her going again.

"Perhaps she's like me, starving, wants a cracker," said Sarah unkindly.

He ducked his head. "I don't believe it," he said an instant later. "I filled her up this morning. You haven't been up to any monkey tricks? No, I see that's impossible. And I used my spare can of gas yesterday."

He stood for a moment looking and listening. Sarah began to laugh, though she suspected there was more hysteria than mirth in the sound. Hunger, fright, desperation, and a measure of disbelief that nothing could allay—murder, battle and sudden death happen to other people, never to oneself—made her feel light-headed.

"Stop that!" said Oliver abruptly. And she stopped.

He turned to the car and wrenched her door open; then he pulled her out. She cried at the pain in her arms.

"This is where we have to take a chance," he told her. "I will say for Madame she doesn't do things by halves."

He took a clasp knife from his pocket and opened the blade. Sarah tried frantically to pull away.

"Stand still, you little fool, I'm not going to cut your throat. What good would it do me to have you found here beside my car, to say nothing of ruining my own clothes? Cutting throats is a very messy affair."

"I'll take your word for it. And, of course, it would be dreadful to spoil your suit." He grabbed her hand. "Come on, we're going down."

She looked over the edge; the ground seemed to drop sheer into a nest of treetops. "No," she cried, pulling back with all her strength.

"If I have to carry you we shall both crash," he told her. She really had no choice. If she refused she was convinced he would knock her on the head, whereas on the way down her chance might come. "There's a path here; granted it's steep, but other men have used it. We can go down sensibly or you can pitch us both into eternity. I don't recommend the latter."

She looked down at her feet. "I can't walk in these slippers," she protested. "They're like sabots."

"Then walk without them," he said brutally. With a violent lunge he had pulled her over the edge; his free hand caught the trunk of a tree, which took their combined weight. His method seemed to be to slide down the path, dragging her after him till a convenient tree blocked the road, and then lie up against it. One of her slippers came off at once, her cheek was scratched by branches, her stockings were torn. She tried to snatch at treetrunks herself and delay their descent, but she was no match for him, and in any case the feeling was only returning slowly to her arms, which felt as useless as matchsticks.

"Stop!" she cried at last. "You must stop a minute. I've cut my ankle."

Her breath came in sobbing gasps; blood flowed from a deep scratch where she had stumbled over an old root. The world seemed marvelously still, not even a bird called. Then, as Oliver, impatient, stooped to examine the damage, she heard it, the sound he had heard that had sent him pell-mell over the edge, despite all the perils of the descent. Somewhere a car was climbing the hill. It was panting almost as much as she did herself; it moved slowly, but it moved. And cars don't drive themselves. She began to laugh, an odd, jangled sound. Instantly Oliver's hand came over her mouth and she remembered the instant outside the villa when she turned the corner calling Johnny's name and a hand came out to silence her.

"Keep still," Oliver said.

She exerted every last ounce of strength and lunged herself against him. One arm was wrapped securely around a tree; he had loosened his own hold to see what damage had been done to the ankle, and she caught him off balance. She stood there, horrified despite her relief, unbelieving, watching his body turning till it was lost among the treetops. She remembered the view from the top of the road; he wouldn't have a chance. "It was him or me," she said, panting and wondering why she was talking aloud since there was no one else there. But she couldn't feel truimph at having outwitted him, gratitude that she had at last a chance to save herself; she could only think that by this act she had put herself on a level with Martin and Madame Auberon, cold-blooded plotters . . .

"I really am going mad," she told herself fiercely. "Most likely he's only broken a leg or something; someone will find him."

The car was coming closer. The side of the hill looked like a cliff; it seemed impossible she had ever got so far down, imposible that she should ever get back. She put her hands to her mouth and shouted. She heard the echoes ringing through the still air. Surely whoever came would see the car, would stop and wonder what on earth it was doing there. At that place on the road it would be possible to pass. All the trees about her seemed to take up the cry. She couldn't believe it when she heard the car drawing to a halt.

Clutching at the nearest tree she hoisted herself a few steps upward. The sun was in her eyes now, the day was drawing on; darkness seemed to come earlier in these woods. Foot by foot she moved upward toward the golden glow. Then something whistled in the air; a rope fell toward her. She caught it in her free hand. Stout though it was, it didn't seem strong enough to hold her if she let go of the supporting tree. Someone was shouting instructions. They didn't seem to make much sense, but she must have followed them, because suddenly she was quite near the top. Arms came out to catch her, to draw her over the edge; she stood trembling, perspiration pouring into her eyes. She was surprised to find she had come up some distance beyond the Panther, clutching and tearing at any convenient growth. A hand opened a car door; someone helped her in.

"Don't try and talk, not for a minute, you've had a shock. Did you fall or . . . ?"

She muttered, "He fell," but perhaps her companion didn't hear. At all events his chief concern seemed to be with her. Her concern was not to black out; she felt like someone staggering on the threshold of an unknown world.

"Lie still, we can get some brandy soon," the voice said. She had an odd feeling she had heard it somewhere before. All the trees were beginning to whirl together now, and the sound of the motor seemed to conflict with the fierce beating of her heart. She thought perhaps it was good advice to lie still for a few minutes.

They were proceeding smoothly along the road, beginning to descend. The light was paling, the world seemed altogether more normal; it was difficult to believe she had pushed Oliver down the hill.

"I pushed him," she said suddenly.

"Good for you," said the driver.

"No. How could it be? But it was my one chance."

"That's why it was good."

"I don't know what you're talking about," she said. "Where are you taking me? Where is this place?"

"You'll see," he said. He turned. The sun was right off his

face now. And he was no stranger, though a week before she had never set eyes on him. The last time she had seen that face had been in the garden of the villa when she went out to call Johnny in.

"Neat of you to push him overboard," said the voice smoothly as the elderly black car proceeded on its way. "I'd have been glad to do it myself. Do you know what he did to *her*?" His voice sank; there was a note of savagery in it that made Sarah shrink back in her place. "Bound and gagged her, left her there like a trussed chicken. She could have suffocated for all he cared, and probably would have if I hadn't come by about fifteen minutes later."

She said, her head swimming, "You're talking about Madame Auberon, the one I thought was Mrs. Abercrombie." And plucking up her courage she added, "What made you do that? Where is Mrs. Abercrombie?"

"Why, at Biarritz I suppose, or wherever her friend's yacht is at this moment. Where should she be?"

"I don't know. I was asking you. Let me ask you something else? Why did you bring me here?"

"Because you talk too much, you talk to everyone."

"But how could anything I say do you any harm?"

There was no reply so Sarah tried another tack. "How did you know where to look for us?"

"The tire treads of a Panther are fairly distinctive. I simply had to follow his trail."

"You know all the answers, don't you? Perhaps you can tell me who he really is."

"Who who really is?"

"The one who calls himself Oliver Abercrombie."

"How should I know? Is there any reason why he shouldn't be Oliver Abercrombie?"

"But he's dead. The lawyer . . ."

"Mistakes have been made before. Anyway, it doesn't matter any more, does it?"

"But it does," she cried. "You must go back, you must find him, he'll be hurt."

"Oh, he'll be past that," said Martin callously.

"It's my fault," she said. "He kept telling me he was on my side, that what he was doing was for my good, and I didn't believe him."

She lay back once again. Martin had fallen silent; she knew it was no good asking where they were going, yet she did ask. "Are we going back to Les Hirondelles?"

"What do you think? If he knew you were there . . ."

Her heart leaped up. If Oliver had known, wasn't it possible that Johnny knew—or Crook himself? What had Oliver said? *I know about Crook.* She lay silent at last, whispering his name over and over, like a litany—"Crook"—"Crook"—"Crook."

II

After Martin's departure from Les Hirondelles to follow the track of Oliver's car, Madame Auberon became exceedingly busy.

"I'll deal with Oliver and the girl," Martin had said. "You get packed, remove all traces of her from the cottage and wait for me to call you. I'll tell you where to meet me."

"Why trouble about them?" Françoise Auberon had pleaded. "Let Oliver have her, let them go to the police; for that matter, let the police come here. We can be gone . . ."

"Not in daylight," said Martin. "Besides, Raoul won't have the boat till tonight. Bring only what you can carry; it may not be possible for me to bring the car round to the house. That man, Crook, is asking questions, and there's the young Englishman from the garage."

"The girl is what you call a quick worker," observed Madame Auberon dryly.

"The girl is nothing to us. All the same, she must not be allowed to tell her story. Now Françoise, remember what I have said. Answer no telephones, open no doors, at all events not until after dark."

"What are you proposing to do, Martin?"

"We cannot afford to leave witnesses behind us; the girl must be persuaded not to speak. I think I know a way. Now, you are expecting no one?"

"I was not expecting Oliver Abercrombie."

"How long a start have they?" Martin inquired.

"They had been gone about fifteen minutes when you came."

"And he drove the large car?"

"There was a car in the lane . . ."

"I wish I knew where he was proposing to take her. Still, it shouldn't be difficult to pick up the trail. There is not much traffic on this road."

She stood a moment at the door, watching him drive away. She looked at her watch. Five hours at least, she thought. Much can happen in five hours. The next thing that happened to her was the arrival of the police.

The sergeant had been on duty at the St. Crécy station when he was called to the telephone. An anonymous voice said, "There is a woman bound and gagged in a house on the Ferrancourt Road. The house is called Les Hirondelles. Someone should go over there."

"Who is speaking?" the sergeant demanded.

"Someone who doesn't want her to suffocate. She is not young. The door is unlatched, you should have no trouble." And the mysterious caller hung up on him.

"If he knows about her," inquired his wondering assistant, "why does he not untie her himself?"

"You, a policeman, to ask me that?" snapped Louis. "Because he is the one who tied her up, of course. You note he did not say how long ago this was. He has no wish to stand trial for murder or even for manslaughter. Who lives at this house, Les Hirondelles?"

The records confirmed that it was occupied by a Madame

Françoise Auberon; the name meant nothing to the sergeant.

"No doubt she keeps her money on the premises and the word has gone round. Or there is a rumor that she has buried treasure, like that villa at St. Mariole."

"Then there isn't any treasure there?" asked the young policeman in disappointed tones.

"If there is, no one's found it. Why are you waiting? Do you wish to be an accomplice in a case of manslaughter? It's to be hoped we shan't find that we've another corpse on our hands when we get there. The one we dug up at the villa is enough to deal with. This Crook from London is going on in a way fit to bring down the Government. Now, if only *he'd* been abducted . . ."

When they reached Les Hirondelles the place looked neat and unexceptional enough. No one was in the garden, and when they looked through the window of the living room the place was empty.

"Ring the bell," commanded the sergeant testily.

"If she's really bound and gagged—or do you think it is a joke?"

"If that is the way it turns out it will prove no joke to the perpetrator. Ring the bell. If you're going to be a policeman you have to keep your eyes open. Didn't you see a curtain upstairs move as we opened the gate?"

The bell was answered immediately by a comely, fresh-faced woman, who appeared perfectly composed and looked at them inquiringly.

"There is something wrong?" she asked, surprise in her big amber-colored eyes.

"We received a telephone call to say there had been an assault on a woman at this address."

Madame Auberon shook her head. "I live here alone, and you can see for yourself I am neither assaulted nor gagged. Perhaps it is not the right house?"

"It's the house all right," grumbled the sergeant. "Have you had any visitors today, madame?"

"Not so much as a postman. Who told you this story?"

"He didn't leave his name. He appeared to think you might suffocate."

"And—when was this?"

"Naturally we came at once." The sergeant's voice was stiff.

"Perhaps there is method in his madness," said the woman slowly. "If the police are at a remote cottage called Les Hirondelles they cannot be in some other place where they might be needed more."

"She could have something there, Sergeant," said the young policeman. "It has been done before."

"Madame will understand that it is the duty of the police to follow up every story they receive, even though in many cases it seems clear it will prove a waste of time. Someone has reported a gagged prisoner at this address . . ."

Her eyes widened till they resembled toy suns. "You mean, you wish to search my house? But surely, without an order . . ."

"I can get an order," said Louis stolidly. "It's only a formality, but if there had been any truth in this telephone call, you must see that your reaction would be precisely what it is."

Françoise stepped back. "You will be wasting your time," she warned them. "There is no one here except myself, but you are welcome to look."

"You live alone here, madame? You are a widow?"

"I call myself a widow. The last time I saw Monsieur Auberon was more than two years ago in Marseilles. The last time I heard from him was three years ago. We do not meet, we do not correspond. So you will understand why I call myself a widow."

"He has never threatened your safety?"

"In that case I should have come to the police at once. It will not take you very long to examine my house," she added. "There are no secret passages or blocked doors."

Everything looked very fresh and clean, everywhere the attentive sergeant saw traces of good, frugal housekeeping. A woman like that, he thought, has no right to be a widow. But most probably she had her distractions. Had he come from St. Mariole, or consulted his brother, he would have known with a good deal more accuracy what those compensations were, but no word had reached St. Crécy of Martin Ribaud's homework, as Johnny had once described it.

"It is a large house for one woman," the sergeant remarked, as they proceeded from floor to floor, and she showed him various empty rooms. "Are you always alone?"

"Sometimes during the season I have the occasional visitor —just for room and breakfast, you understand. I do not run a pension or advertise for guests, but sometimes I am asked for a bed—young men walking who have missed their way, travelers whose cars are being repaired at the nearest garage —who could refuse them?"

The sergeant nodded. He understood. She rented the occasional room, provided the occasional meal for small amounts which never appeared on her tax papers. She held no license as a boarding-house keeper; the small sums she took could hardly be regarded as income. It happened everywhere, a small matter not worth the time and expense of the police to follow it up. A deserted wife turning the odd ten francs—all public sympathy would be with her. He looked around keenly for signs of male occupancy in any of the rooms but there was none. Yet it was hard to believe a woman like this would live alone, as chaste as a mission sister. His race had always been opposed to waste, and he put her age at around forty.

She accompanied the authorities on their deliberate and systematic search of the house, wearing the same cool smile of assurance, the smile of one who knows there is nothing to find. And, in fact, there was no one on the ground floor, no one in the backyard, no one anywhere. He had to admit himself baffled.

From Les Hirondelles he called the police station, but there was no news of an alarming kind. If the call had been a trick, it seemed a remarkably purposeless one.

Madame politely asked them to come to the kitchen—a small glass of something—and they agreed. She told them she intended shortly to put the house on the market; she was leaving to share quarters with a cousin, newly bereaved. The sergeant commented on a number of theatrical photographs on the walls.

"Yourself, madame?"

"Naturally," said Madame with a smile.

She had had great ambitions as a girl, she said; had traveled with touring theatrical companies—"That is where I learned to speak English," she explained, "and it is useful to me now. Some of my occasional young men speak only English."

Without a word spoken Louis contrived to suggest that some of them at least doubtless spoke the language of love. Under Madame's smiling and approving eye he seemed to unshrivel; you could almost see him blossom. The young policeman watched him, open-mouthed. Who would ever have thought it of glum, prickly Louis Grasse?

The police were reluctantly on the point of leaving when there came another interruption, this time infinitely more dramatic. A big bright yellow car rushed down the road and stopped at their gate. Two men hopped out: one looking big enough to sweep the cottage into the sea—it was one of Crook's gifts that at a first meeting he always appeared taller than he was; the other, a younger man, with a face as full of hope as a tombstone.

"Mr. Crook!" exclaimed the sergeant.

"I warned you we'd be meeting again one of these days. I'm here on the same lay as yourself," he went on. "Want to ask the lady a few questions. *Parlez anglais?*" His big brown eyes met Françoise's furious amber-colored gaze. She swept the question aside like a bit of dust you sweep into a pan.

"Who is this person?" she demanded of the sergeant. "What is he doing here?"

"It's like I said, I've come to ask a few questions—about Sugar—Miss Hollis to you. Understand you met at the villa Tuesday night."

Françoise turned to the sergeant, addressing him in a spate of French that seemed to the slower English tongue enough to brush him off into eternity.

"Don't let her fool you," Crook advised. "Here, Johnny, you do the interpreting. Let the sergeant know this ain't the first time Madame's heard my name. Martin will have seen to that."

Johnny and the sergeant embarked on a sort of spitting match. Then Johnny said, "He wants to know if you're the chap who rang up and told them to come here to untie a captive."

"That was Oliver. Rang from some mountain hut. Sorry to cause the lady any inconvenience, he said, but he had to be sure of getting Sugar away. Then he rang me and sent me along here to get proof."

"Proof of what?" demanded Madame scornfully.

"That she'd been here, of course. Daresay by now you've wiped away most traces, but Oliver had to be sure there was proof."

"Who is this Oliver?" Madame demanded.

"As if you didn't know! Oliver Abercrombie. According to him he's the rightful owner of the villa, but the legal beagles can fight that one out." He looked at her thoughtfully. "You talk English very nice. Acting around the world, I suppose."

"Why should you suppose this Oliver was ever in my house?" Madame continued.

"We rather thought you might play it that way. Well, someone had to have kidnaped Sugar in the first place. It wasn't me, it wasn't the curé, it wasn't Johnny here. That only left Oliver and Martin, and Oliver convinced me it wasn't him. If it was Martin he had to put the girl somewhere, and he had three choices. I didn't somehow think he'd take her to Marie at Lourdes—the son-in-law might have asked some awkward questions. He could, of course, have left her in the woods—that was a chance we were bound to consider—or he could have brought her here."

"He was taking a chance, wasn't he?" snapped the sergeant.

"Maybe he thought Madame here wouldn't be so anxious

for his company if she knew he'd killed a girl who stood in his way. I mean, it's always easier the second time. Maybe he meant to turn Sugar adrift in the woods when him and Madame had made their getaway. By the time she struggled back to what passes for civilization hereabouts they'd be where the law couldn't touch 'em. There's still countries where the extradition law don't operate."

Madame shrugged her shoulders. She might have retired from the stage, but she could still put on a pretty good act.

"So Martin and I were to abandon our homes and live free as air—and on air?" she suggested. "Martin is a working man . . ."

"Well yes," Crook agreed, "that had occurred to me, too. That's what makes me think he must have laid hands on the treasure. Well, there had to be some good reason for the murder of Mrs. Abercrombie." Françoise Auberon turned in a flash.

"What is that—about murder? What are you saying? You are crazy. Madame is at Biarritz with her friends . . ." She turned to the sergeant. "You cannot believe a word this man says."

"She really does believe what she told us about Mrs. A.," Crook agreed. "She really does."

The sergeant broke in, wildly impatient, to know what all this was about. Crook and Johnny both tried to tell him. In other circumstances the situation would have been wildly funny: Crook waving his arms and hamming it up, Madame expostulating first in one tongue then in the other, the police constable, Michel, putting in his oar—this was his first murder and what a start!—Johnny trying to make the sergeant understand the facts.

"Facts!" shouted Louis Grasse, becoming as excited as the rest. "Whose facts? Yours? Mr. Crook's? Madame's? Or the absent Oliver Abercrombie's?"

Crook said simply, "You do appreciate what it must have been like at the Tower of Babel. Look, Johnny, you tell the law there's one point we can settle easy, and that's if Sugar was ever here. According to Oliver, he left a clue under a black wooden cupboard thing on an upper landing."

"Almost every house hereabouts has such a cupboard," said Madame, still in something of a daze. "I can assure you . . ."

"Simple enough to find out, isn't it?" Crook suggested. "If the clue ain't there Oliver's a liar. What say we all go up and take a look-see? Four witnesses—well, five, including Madame—must be four times as good as one."

The bewildered and angry sergeant, the intent constable, Johnny shaking with apprehension, Crook looking his usual self, followed Françoise up the stairs.

"What is the nature of this clue, monsieur?" Louis inquired of Johnny, whose reply was interrupted.

"Tell him its a little goldy earring shaped like a bell, and the other one was still on Sugar's ear when Oliver last sighted her."

Michel rootled under the cupboard, Crook said helpfully he had a flashlight, Madame stood rigid as a statue hemmed in by the two Englishmen. After a minute Michel stood up, his hand outstretched. On the palm was a small gold earring shaped like a bell.

"Sugar'll be glad to have that back," Crook observed. "I remember thinking how nice they looked that evening we first met."

"She was wearing them the day I met her, too," Johnny contributed. "Quite unusual, aren't they?"

Madame shrugged impatiently. "No doubt such trinkets are turned out by the thousand," she declared.

"Then maybe you can show us the other half of this pair," Crook offered. "And at the same time you might explain how it is that a lady whose ears are pierced comes to have a clip-on earring under her clothespress."

"You don't miss much, do you?" said Johnny.

"The minute you stop noticing, that's the minute the other chap steps in with his blunt instrument. That was Oliver's mistake "

"Where is Oliver now?" Johnny asked. "Isn't he with Sarah?"

"Now don't take it too hard. Oliver's a resourceful fellow, but even resourceful fellows can't always tell the working of the female mind. You'd have thought any dame would be grateful to her savior, as it were, winkling her out of the prison den, but not Sugar. No, she knew all the answers. Oliver was the big bad wolf, in cahoots with Martin and the lady here. Mind you, he had a lot on his mind, or he might have been able to persuade her—but you never can tell. He came along here looking for Sugar and I waited to hear the result. He rang me, like I said, from this eyrie on the cliff somewhere or other the same time as he called to tell the police about Madame."

"The police will tell you that when they arrived I had been neither assaulted nor gagged," Madame insisted.

"That can only be because Martin got here ahead of them. That's what Oliver was afraid of, Martin jumping out on him at any minute. His job was to put Sugar where she'd be safe, so he took her off up the mountain path, and then his luck went back on him; he ran out of petrol. Hadn't allowed for how much the Panther'ud eat making that climb, I suppose, unless one of the chaps at the garage siphoned off some of the gasoline overnight. It's been done before. He was planning to go back to the eyrie and phone a garage when he heard the sound of a car following up the path. Mind you, he couldn't swear it was Martin, but there ain't many cars come that way, and he couldn't afford to take any chances. Far as we know, Martin's still got the gun and we know he don't scruple to use it. The bullet in Mrs. Abercrombie was fired from behind. Must have given her the shock of her life if she had time to feel anything."

"That is the second time you have said Madame Abercrombie has been shot," Françoise put in.

"Ask the sergeant here. He was there when we found her. And Martin admitted the old lady used to have a gun. Swore he'd thrown it away a long while back, of course, but you don't have to believe everything you hear. Oliver knew about it, and he hadn't gone to all that trouble for Sugar to get a bullet in *her* back, so he invited her to do a bit of rock-climbing—no, rock-climbing in reverse. It was tricky, but it seemed the lesser of two evils. Only Sugar was like the greyhound in the poem; she hung back and checked him in his leap."

Johnny said in sudden shocked tones, "Where's Oliver now?"

"If it was you or me we'd be in a refrigerated box waiting for the coroner to give the say-so for burial," Crook told him. "Lucky for Oliver he was brought up in a circus."

Madame snorted with derision. "A circus indeed! What sort of talk is this?"

"True as I stand here," said Crook. "Well, why not? We're most of us in one sort of circus or other. His father fled to the States after the First World War, couldn't take life at the villa hemmed in by exclusive saints. He found a job in a circus. Oliver was born and brought up there; left it after he saw his mum break her back falling from a trapeze. No regulations about nets in that outfit; public get a bigger thrill if there's a chance of a fatality. Anyway, Oliver opted out, but he ain't forgotten his early training. When Sugar gave him a hearty shove and he felt himself falling he went automatically into his routine. Seems you have to be flexible so you don't break anything when you fall. Like gelatine."

The sergeant interposed. "He wants to know how you know all this," Johnny said.

"He had a bit of luck—Oliver, I mean—didn't fall the whole way, managed to land on one of the paths and clutch at the undergrowth. And then," he added simply, "he just walked up the hill again. And don't tell me he couldn't because that's what he did. Went back to the eyrie and rang me, and I got in touch with a garage who're sending a tow-away truck to fetch the Panther."

"Wouldn't it have served the same purpose if they'd just sent out some gasoline?" asked Johnny dryly.

"Oliver was playing safe this time. For all he knew Martin had stopped to put the Panther out of action, so even if by some miracle Oliver or one of his mates got back to her it wouldn't do him much good. A little fiddle with the brakes at a place like that, and even Oliver couldn't save himself if he went over the edge when he was inside a car. Or he could have let the air out of the tires—anything."

"And what about Sarah?" demanded Johnny, sounding demented. "Why didn't you tell me all this before?"

"Because there's nothing you could do till we proved this point. Oliver's word might satisfy me; it wasn't going to satisfy the police. Oliver's going along to see the Inspector, and he'll set the wires humming."

"And Sarah is back in Martin's power?"

"Speaking for myself, I'd as soon have a crocodile on my track as Oliver Abercrombie. Oh, there's nothing half-hearted about him, and a chap who'll let a girl push him overboard and come up for more means business.

"Now, one more word in the sergeant's ear before we go. The late Mrs. Abercrombie's trunks, the ones she was to take to Biarritz, weren't in the villa, and it don't seem likely Martin's careering round the country with them in the trunk of his car. I spied a kind of cupboard-thing upstairs there, might be interesting to run over and see what's inside."

With this kindly thought he left the protesting sergeant. "We've got to be back on the job," he explained, "and our job is Sugar. Mrs. Abercrombie could get herself murdered six days a week for me and I wouldn't lift a finger. Who am I to do the police out of their daily bread? We've got to get back to St. Crécy and see how the cookie crumbles at that end. Leave Madame to the right authorities. Oh, and Oliver has the notion she may have used a hypo on our girl. It 'ud snarl everything up if she had the chance now to use it on herself."

The sergeant was still protesting when they left. "Tell you

who I wouldn't be," said Crook, "and that's Martin when Marie finds out he was planning to run off with the widow. To say nothing of the treasure."

"You don't even know he has the treasure," Johnny protested. "We don't even know if it existed."

"There had to be some good reason for murder," Crook told him. "My guess 'ud be they did find the treasure, Martin and Marie, and somehow Madame got onto them. Could have threatened them with the police—I don't know. Of course, anyone with one hundred percent intelligence would have called the police first, but dames are creatures of impulse. And Oliver will go along with that."

"What did you mean when you said Oliver meant business?" Johnny demanded.

"Well, I don't think he's in this for his health. And he ain't doing it for gratitude, because Sugar ain't giving him any. Mind you," he took a corner neatly, "if it was me I'd go for the more homely type, but then he's used to a bit of excitement, probably appreciates the idea of a wife with some spirit. Now come, we're not going to have any of the little green-eyed monster, surely. How old are you?"

"Twenty-two," said Johnny.

"In a position to support a wife? I thought not. Lucky, I daresay, if you can keep yourself. And the ladies aren't like us. They like things dainty. No milk bottles on the table for them, and beer out of a glass. No, you take second place this time, offer to be the best man, and you'll find it's a case of the chap on the sidelines seeing most of the game."

"Sarah once told me I was as gossipy as a spinster," exploded Johnny. "Just let her wait till she gets to know you a bit better."

"That's all I want," said Crook earnestly. "Believe me, Johnny boy, that's all I want."

The car sped on into St. Crécy.

12

At the police station there was nothing new to report. Inspector Bertin had sent for reinforcements from neighboring villages, a watch was being kept on all roads, cars being stopped, a warning put out about this particular car.

"Martin might have ditched it and hired himself a self-drive," Crook explained.

"Or ditched Sarah."

"Or ditched Sarah," Crook agreed steadily. "Point is, does he know we've found Madame Abercrombie where he dumped *her?* You know, Madame Auberon's shock when we told her about the murder was no act. Going to the ends of the earth with a chap who's already put one dame underground is about as safe as putting your head in the tiger's mouth. Bluebeard may have been a charmer to the ends of his fingernails, but only a moron would have wanted to string along with him once she knew the secret of his locked room. You know, if it wasn't that Sugar was involved, I could almost be sorry for Martin. What's that text—'Mine deadly enemies, who compass me about'—the police, Oliver, you, me, Marie . . ."

"You'll have me crying in a minute," said Johnny dryly. "Who is Oliver really? Don't tell me you haven't solved that little problem yet."

"Could *be* Oliver Abercrombie. Yes, I know about him being dead and buried two years ago, but a chap who can fall down a precipice and come back not much the worse for wear ain't going to be floored by a little thing like a tombstone."

"Suppose Martin hasn't got her?" suggested Johnny. "Had you thought of that?"

"Of course I'd thought of that. Only, if not, where is she? And where's Martin? Oliver don't think it's likely she could have climbed back on her own, though it's amazin' what you can do when your life depends on it. There wasn't any sign of the car when he got back, nor the girl. She might have scrambled down and be wandering round the woods on her own, in which case she wouldn't be much better off. They go on for miles, and the whole of the Metropolitan Police Force couldn't guarantee to find a body there. No news that Martin's ditched the car; my idea is he'll be lying low till dark, then he'll make his way back through the woods near the cottage. He's got to join up with Madame somewhere."

"Unless he ditches her, too."

"Who said there's no fury like a woman scorned? If Madame Auberon realizes he's left her behind to face the music, she might start singing like a canary bird. Marie'll do that in any case," he added. "Don't ask me how I know. I do. I've met her. Besides, you don't take all these risks for a dame if she don't mean something to you. And if he don't go back to Auberon"—here Crook clinched his argument—"how in thunder are we ever going to get on his trail?"

"So what do we do next?"

"I'll tell you what we don't do, and that's put all our eggs in one basket. The police are going to watch the coast in case Martin tries to make a break for it. Airlines—airports, that is—are bein' alerted—garages, bars, the lot. You're going to string along with them. If they do find Sugar she's going to need one familiar face if she's not to go right over the edge, and you're the one she'll trust. Well, naturally. She never tried to push you into eternity, did she?"

"And Oliver?"

"We're going to reconnoiter on our own account, not gettin' under the police's feet. After all, the sea washes up on two sides of the French coast; could be he'll try and make a break the other way, and Oliver can help me there. What worries me most of all," he confessed, "is that Martin's still got that gun, and take my word, he won't scruple to use it."

The plan already forming in Crook's head, that he prudently did not confide to Johnny, was so crazy that any reasonable man—a police inspector, say—would have laughed himself black in the face. But though Crook might have fallen down on some highbrow law examination, he was second to none when it came to knowing about folk, and he was backing his hunch about them now. Suppose we fail? Johnny had asked, but the Bloomsbury lawyer knew that only millionaires can afford failure, and he wasn't in that class.

Meanwhile the old-fashioned black car had left the upper road and was snaking cautiously through the woods that appeared to go on forever.

"Where are you taking me?" demanded Sarah, more because the silence was getting on her nerves than because she expected any useful information.

"We're going to the coast," said Martin agreeably. "You'll like that, won't you?"

"I'd much sooner go back to the villa."

"You can't go there," said Martin. "It's in the hands of the police."

"Why should I care? They're probably looking for me anyway."

"Oh yes," Martin agreed. "You've got everyone by the heels. Mrs. Abercrombie won't be too pleased."

"You mean the real Mrs. Abercrombie."

"I didn't know there was more than one."

"There's the phony I met on Tuesday evening. The one at Les Hirondelles. I still don't understand why you let me go on thinking that."

"You ask too many questions," said Martin.

"I might ask fewer if I had some answers. What is all this cloak-and-dagger business?"

"You answer one of my questions," the man said. "Did you speak to my wife?"

"Marie rang up from Lourdes; she thought you'd be at the villa."

"What did you tell her?"

"That you'd had trouble with the car and missed the train. I didn't know why you hadn't gone to Lourdes, but I said you'd telephone."

"You see?" said Martin. "You make trouble wherever you go."

"You should have explained who she was—Madame Auberon, I mean. How was I to guess the real Mrs. Abercrombie had left for Biarritz that morning? Though I do remember the curé saying he'd met you in the village and you told him you'd just taken her in."

"He misunderstood. And as for an explanation to you . . ." Martin shrugged. "You were never going to meet the real Mrs. Abercrombie. You'd be back in England before her return."

"Which makes it all the more mysterious that you should be so anxious to prevent my meeting anyone. Is it something to do with her? Where is she really?" Martin said nothing. "You wouldn't be running these risks if it wasn't a matter of life and death. There are too many people on my side. Is that it?" She could feel the color draining out of her face. "Is it a matter of life and death? *Your* death?"

"Do you remember what happened to Bluebeard's wife?"

"She looked through a keyhole and saw a body. Oh no! You can't mean she's there, in the locked room, and you hadn't had time to move her before I arrived? Only in that case you'd simply have to watch for me to go out and then break in, if you hadn't got a key."

"I told you, I drove Mrs. Abercrombie into Pau on Tuesday morning."

"Yes, I remember. There was a story I read once, by Walter de la Mare, about a man who drove through a village in the dusk with a woman in the passenger seat. She was noticed and identified by the clothes she wore. She didn't call out or wave or do any of the things she usually did, because she couldn't. They never did find her body. Will anyone find Mrs. Abercrombie's?"

"It mightn't be a bad idea to gag you," said Martin coolly. "How do you expect me to drive with all that yammering going on behind me? Only I'll need your help quite soon."

She uttered a wild snort of laughter. "What makes you think it's going to be as easy as that?"

"This," said Martin, half turning in his place and opening a hand he had just thrust into his pocket. She saw the wicked little gun.

"You don't leave much to chance, do you? Your gun, Madame's hypodermic syringe. Did you use that on *her*?"

Whether he had or not, there was no doubt in her mind that he was prepared to use it now. She lay back, very still. Now fear possessed her; she had always hoped an emergency would find her a heroine. Skill, courage, enterprise, those were the virtues she had secretly believed she would display. And here she was, shaking in her one slipper—she had lost the other on that nightmare descent—realizing at last that murder on the small screen or the printed page is one thing, and the reality, when you're at the receiving end of a gun, something quite different. She had been buoying herself up with thoughts of Crook, of Johnny, even of the police, but a gun made Martin more powerful than any of them. She recalled vaguely that in France the police are armed, but they might not be prepared for Martin to have a weapon and by the time they discovered it, it could be too late.

"Now, listen," said Martin, "we're in this together. When the police know the facts they'll be after you just the same as they are after me. You've killed a man, remember, or done your best."

"It was self-defense," she whispered. "I didn't know . . ."

"That's what they all say. It won't help you much in court. The only person who can help you now is me, and I'm prepared to do it in exchange for a bit of coöperation from you. I could turn you out of the car now—you'd never find your way back—or I could report you to the authorities, and then see how much they'd credit your story. Or I could take you to the coast, and out of France, where they won't think of looking for you."

"That's absurd and you know it." She tried to speak vigorously, but her voice still came out hoarse and strained. "How could I leave the country without a passport, to say nothing of luggage?"

"That can be attended to. Now, are you going to play ball?"

Play for time, insisted her subconscious. Give Crook a chance—Johnny too—you've made enough of a mess of things as it is.

"What do you want me to do?"

"We're going to stop in a minute and do some telephoning."

"We? Or you?"

"I said we. Just remember I'll be at your side all the time, and I'll have this"—once more he indicated the gun—"jammed against your ribs. And don't think I wouldn't use it."

"Who are we going to telephone?"

"You'll find out. And don't think you can be clever. I'll tell you what to say and you'll say it, word for word, or else."

"You—you're not going to ring Marie?" she suggested, and was amazed at the fury with which he exclaimed, "Ring that murdering bitch? Haven't you understood anything? No, I am not going to ring my wife."

So, of course, it had to be Madame Auberon and, of course, it was. In a ghostly way history was repeating itself. Oliver had stopped the car near a bistro and called—who? Crook presumably, perhaps Johnny also, if he knew anything about Johnny. Now here was Martin pulling up near a noisy wayside café and pushing her ahead of him in the direction of the telephone. Some kind of mechanical music was blaring out, a tableful of students were singing, there was a clatter of glasses and plates. Every few minutes a noisy motorcycle started up or sounded its horn. You could fire a shot without anyone suspecting a thing and make your getaway before the body was found by the next person wanting to use the phone.

Martin pushed her up against the wall, one arm about her, the little gun jabbing her ribs.

"When I give you the receiver," he said, "you will say, 'Is that you, Françoise? This is Berthe Roche. I am hoping it may be possible for me to see you tonight.' "

"Why don't you say it yourself?" muttered Sarah.

"Because I don't know the lay of the land." Martin's voice was crisp as a cracker. "Your friend, Oliver may have made trouble for her in official quarters."

He dialed a number and they could hear the bell ringing. It rang for so long it began to seem probable that Françoise was not at the cottage.

"Perhaps you should try the police station," suggested Sarah nastily, and bit back a cry as he viciously slammed the gun into her side. "Now, she is here." The receiver was thrust into her hand. "Remember you are a *French* citizen," he said, hissing.

Obediently she went into her act. "Françoise! This is Berthe Roche."

Françoise spoiled things by asking, "Who is that?"

"You remember Berthe Roche? I was hoping I might see you tonight. It is important, a matter of life and death," she ad-libbed recklessly.

"Dear Berthe!" said the voice, now perfectly under control. "How you exaggerate. And alas! Tonight is out of the question."

"Ask her why?" muttered Martin in her ear.

"You have company?" Sarah suggested.

And Françoise laughed. "Yes, Berthe, I have company. This is the big laugh, though not so amusing for us. There is a policeman here."

"You've got a policeman there?" repeated Sarah for Martin's benefit.

"They are looking for a mad creature who has escaped. All passengers along this road are being stopped, and they will not allow anyone to leave their houses."

"But who is this mad creature who is so dangerous?" Sarah insisted.

"There is talk of murder. That is all I can say except that no visitors can come to the cottage tonight. I am sorry, Berthe, perhaps some other time . . ."

There was a slight sound of scuffling and then a man's voice came along the line.

"Who is that?"

"Are you the police? My name is Berthe Roche, I had hoped to see Madame Auberon this evening, but she says she will be prevented. At least let me say good-bye to her."

But the receiver had been hung up at the other end. Martin's face was as hard as a stone.

"Get going," he said. "What on earth happened to your shoes?"

"Your friend fancied them, and the slippers she gave me in exchange aren't a very good fit. I lost one . . ." She realized she was feeling light-headed, and not surprising, seeing it must have been hours since she had had anything to eat. "I'm starving," she said.

"Too bad," said Martin. "We're not stopping here."

"Can't we buy some sandwiches or something? It won't help you if I faint away in the car." (Or would that suit his book? The trouble was she hadn't had a chance to learn his next move and so prepare for it.)

As they passed the counter Martin bought a long French roll sliced down the middle and stuffed with salami; and a package of chocolate. The man who took the money looked no higher than his customers' hands. Show him a picture of the girl missing from the Villa Abercrombie and ask if she had come his way and he would shake his head. "No one of that description, monsieur."

As they turned away Sarah swept a cup off a table, so that it crashed to the ground, but no one paid any attention. Martin hustled her back to the car. He was white with anger.

"I warned you, no tricks. Get behind the wheel and remember, if you feel inclined to make more trouble, this gun has two ends." Meaning he wouldn't have to attract attention by firing; the butt would do a perfectly good job. There was an expression she had read—pistol-whipped. Martin was the type who would enjoy that, in moments of defeat. Obediently she took the driver's place, Martin sitting close, the gun not more than an inch from her side. Surely he wouldn't risk a shot at such close quarters. Not only would it spatter the car with blood; it would drench him also. But then he must know she would take no chances now.

Once the lighted café was left behind, darkness encompassed them once more. Martin directed her into narrower paths—he knew this wooded district as a goat knows its paths up the mountain. The stillness here was alarming. Once an owl swooped by seeking food for its young; around them came the secret snufflings and rustlings of wild creatures whose lives begin when the shadows start to fall. After a short time he allowed her to stop and handed her the sandwich he had bought in the café. Already she was tormenting herself at the thought of a lost opportunity. Somehow I should have attracted attention, she was thinking, but if she had, the first shot would have been for her, and he would have shot his way out, if need be. Until now she had found that sort of thing credible only in films; that it happened in real life and might even happen to her was something she had never had to contemplate.

The sandwich was excellent. I wish I could get them this good in London, she thought, and a pang shot through her at the thought that London was a place she might never see again.

Martin, who seemed impervious to the pangs of hunger, emptied the contents of his pocket onto his knee: a tobacco pouch, a wallet, a letter, a pack of Camels, a folder of matches.

"I could do with a cigarette," said Sarah enviously.

"So that you might dash the burning end into my face?" scoffed Martin. "No, mademoiselle."

"I hadn't thought of that," she confessed.

It seemed that Martin was taking no chances either. One hand still kept the gun pressed close, and presumably he was not adept at rolling a cigarette one-handed. He shook a Camel out of the pack, lighted it awkwardly, and after a draw put it between her lips. In a minute he took it away again and told her to drive on. A new thought occurred to her. She had been wondering how Martin would explain away blood marks in the car, assuming it came to that. But, of course, it would not. He could compel her to leave the car and shoot her down among the trees. Who would hear the sound of a gun in this remote spot, and who knew when her body might be found? And when it is, she told herself, how will it be identified? I haven't even got my watch. She found she was clenching her hands on the wheel. He'll have to shoot them off to make me move, she thought fiercely.

The journey seemed to go on forever. The bright day, when she had left Les Hirondelles in Oliver's company, belonged to another time, another world. They were moving slowly. Time did not seem to matter to him, and he refused to let her put on the lights.

"Suppose I crash into a tree?" she offered, but he only laughed. She hadn't the least notion where they were when she heard, not too far away, the sound of a car.

We can't be far from a road, she thought. She played with the idea of sounding the horn, but her courage failed her, and the sound of the car's motor died in the dark.

"Stop here," said Martin suddenly. And she looked around in surprise. This is it. The words throbbed in her blood. This is it. But once she had applied the brake Martin seemed content to wait. He was watching intently, staring toward the road. Suddenly light dawned.

"We're near Les Hirondelles, we've come round in a circle," she declared. "But this is crazy. You can't really believe she'll come. How can she, with the police on the premises? Or do you imagine she can drug the gendarme as she drugged me?" She had a vision of Françoise, the hypodermic syringe at the ready, hovering around the unsuspecting policeman like some great bee, waiting for its opportunity to sting. The picture was irresistible; she began to laugh. It was like the discordant cry of a jay.

"I told you to stop that," said Martin.

"She told you—it's impossible. Surely you realized she was warning you off?" A fresh idea came into her mind. "Or has *she* got the treasure? Is she bringing it? Well, you'd hardly carry it around in a car the police are looking for."

He said savagely, "Do you suppose I would let her take that risk? Be quiet! She will come."

"And we're all going down to the coast together? You're fooling yourself, you know."

"If she cannot come there will be a message."

"She's already given you the message, over the phone. Anyway, now she knows about Mrs. Abercrombie, perhaps she won't be so keen to come."

"What should she know?"

"She said something about murder. Whose else could it be?"

Now that her eyes were accustomed to the gloom Sarah realized that the dark shadow on the horizon was probably Les Hirondelles. Martin was waiting for a message, but how? Morse code with an electric light? But would the policeman grant her the opportunity? And would Madame, in fact, know the Morse code?

"I don't know the Morse code," she said aloud.

Martin took out his watch. She tried to see the face, but he kept this shielded from her.

"Drive on," he said abruptly. "You are right. She has been prevented."

From this moment his manner changed. Before, it had been pitiless with the ruthlessness of a man who cannot afford compassion. Now it was ferocious in its hate of herself, the police, Crook, anyone who came between him and his love.

"What about Marie?" she heard herself say. "Aren't you afraid she may tell the police?"

He turned his head, like a blind man. "How could she?" he inquired simply.

"Because she's in it, too? Ah, when she realizes you've double-crossed her, she may take the chance. She could plead undue influence. At least English wives can."

"We are not in England, mademoiselle. No, that one will never go to the police. Turn left here," he added. "Soon we shall be on the other road, and remember what I have told you."

Suddenly an immense weakness overwhelmed her; she felt as though her arms had no strength in them. Insensibly her will had begun to weaken also. Why should she obey this monster's orders, drive him to his rendezvous in order to be disposed of in the most cold-blooded manner on arrival? Because now she was certain of his plan. She and Martin and the car would all reach the coast, but only Martin would continue the journey alive.

It wasn't a new gambit, it had often been done before. Since time immemorial cars had been running over cliff paths, diving headlong into a full tide. Accident, coroners said; carelessness, intoxicated drivers, bad roads, poor light. Only this time is wasn't going to be any of these things. The car was going over the cliff at an uninhabited spot after dark, and there need be no expectation here of any miracle. Leave a door open and if questions were asked, why, the driver had been drowned trying to swim for it. The body might be washed up later—much much later—somewhere along the coast. She didn't know how strongly the currents ran hereabouts. And by then the water would have done its work. There would be nothing to identify the swollen, faceless creature she would have become.

"What are you waiting for?" Martin demanded, and she realized that insensibly she had slowed their pace. "Hoping perhaps we shall miss the tide?"

"You and your we's," she said giggling. "If you want to know, I'm dead beat." And she winced, thinking how much better she might have phrased it.

"Up here," Martin said. "We'll be on that road in a minute. There's not likely to be much traffic, but remember what I warned you about. If you get up to any of your monkey tricks . . ."

"Why not?" demanded Sarah. "What have I got to lose?"

But once more an irrational hope moved in her. On a road there was always the chance of traffic, no matter how light. Anything would do—a van, a minicar, even an old dame walking her poodle. Well, perhaps not the old dame. He would have no hesitation about shooting her down. Sarah looked quickly in both directions but there was no one about. People who live in towns and complain of traffic congestion don't know their luck, she thought. There were no dwellings either, and even if there were, the owners would be eating or reading or watching TV, or even making love. Never guessing what was passing in the dark road outside . . . She began to sing:

> While viewers watched their sets by night
> All seated round the flame,
> A car went by without a light,
> And Murder was its name.

"We play that at home sometimes," she told Martin. "It's called Rhyming Off the Cuff. Why don't we sing?" she added recklessly. "It might keep me awake. It won't help either of us if I go to sleep at the wheel and run us off the road.

Though if I had the lion heart with which the English are normally credited, that's just what I would do."

"What do you suggest we should sing?" asked Martin unmoved.

"There must be something we both know." But now that so much might depend upon it, every song title she had ever known eluded her. "Isn't that odd?" she marveled. "I can't remember a single song to save my life."

She broke into fits of the wildest laughter. "Did you hear what I said? It was rather neat—rather neat."

"Stop that!" Martin warned her again. "I don't have to take you as far as the coast, you know."

That sobered her up, gave her a new idea. Granted she was beyond hope, wasn't there something in the old Churchillian dictum that you can always take one with you? Suppose, when they reached the coast, she turned the car off the road and plunged them both into the sea? She could think of men whose company she would prefer in the hour of death, but nobody can win them all.

They rounded a corner and she looked hopefully ahead, but people did not seem to live along this road. All she could see was a long tumble-down barn affair where once perhaps sheep had been kept, probably before the road was made, and where now derelict hikers or outcasts crept for a night's shelter.

" 'While shepherds watched their flocks by night,' " she sang, but petered out after the first line.

"You can put on the lights now," Martin said. The first thing they showed up was what looked like a lump of mud lying in the path of the car; she stood on the brakes.

"What now?"

"A toad," she explained. "It's unlucky to run down a toad, as well as inhuman."

"You stopped the car for a toad?"

"It's all right, it's got out of the way now. We used to have a toad on the porch of our house when I was a little girl. How much farther?"

"You'll see."

"Why make a road if no one uses it?" she asked. "All right, you don't have to answer. I'm just talking to keep myself awake. . . . *What's that?*" Behind them a car horn had set up a steady, insistent blare.

13

When the old black car had rounded the bend of the road, an even older model, painted bright yellow, came grumbling out of the derelict shed and followed in the black car's wake.

If the vigil had seemed long to Sarah it had appeared endless to Crook. The only thing he could feel thankful for was that Johnny was with the police, who would keep him under supervision. The last time Crook saw him he was fit to be tied. Crook had clung to his original theory that Martin would try to call at Les Hirondelles for Madame Auberon. He had driven the Superb past the cottage and seen a discreet light in the front window. He had no doubt that Françoise was still inside. He tooled past, keeping his eyes skinned for a light moving through the woods. When he saw none he refused to lose heart; Martin was capable of driving blind. He may not have the girl with him, Crook had told Oliver, and if it turned out that he did not, there was only one answer to the question of what had happened. The real problem here would be where did it happen? Sooner or later, he argued, the chap is bound to come out of the woods. Common sense will tell him he will have a reception party waiting for him at the St. Mariole end; his one chance is to make for Collioure or some other point on the eastern side.

Under the trees the shadows lay like black velvet and any one of them might conceal a body. But Crook took heart from the fact that he had heard nothing that could have been a shot; the sound would carry a long way on such a still night. And then when he felt, despite the evidence of his big turnip watch, it must be nearly morning, he saw a light moving, unhurried but definite, in the dark maze of the trees a little way ahead. Dousing his own lights he kept pace with the car until he saw the old barn, which promised an excellent vantage point. And he heard something more beautiful to him than the angel chorus on Christmas morning. He heard a girl's voice singing, and he knew he still had a chance. He put his car back into gear, gave his quarry the briefest of starts and came into action, hooting like a maniac.

"What the hell's that?" exclaimed Martin. "I didn't see the light of a car."

"Perhaps the battery failed," Sarah suggested. "Or perhaps it's someone like ourselves who's trying to escape notice."

"Making that din?" demanded Martin.

"He sounds as though he wants to pass," Sarah offered.

"Then draw in and let him go by." The road here was wide enough to take two cars, provided both drivers were sober.

"Or perhaps," Sarah continued, speaking in a high, light voice, he's trying to attract our attention. Martin leaned across her and imperiously waved the other driver on. But no one came past.

"Look!" whispered Sarah. From the distant lower road a light became visible, a light like a fallen star; then, like mountain answering to mountain, a second horn began to sound. The little light began to climb steadily.

"Step on it!" Martin ordered, his voice rising to a shout. "Go through him, if necessary." Then as she seemed to hesitate, he added ominously, "The safety catch is off, if that means anything to you."

The black car shook with the suddenness of its leap forward. Sarah put her finger on the horn and hooted in her turn.

"We must warn him. We don't want to be cut in two," she explained. For all his threats, she was convinced Martin would not shoot now—he couldn't spare the time. He must be cursing himself that it was she who was behind the wheel. He was jammed against her, his arm around her shoulders held her rigid. The black car bounced and shot from side to side of the uneven road. Below them the path fell away to black woodland. "Push her on," Martin insisted.

"You'll have us both over the edge, provided none of the tires bursts," Sarah warned him. Martin was in a real jam now. He couldn't turn the car off the road; there was nowhere for it to go that did not spell destruction. He had no doubt now about his situation. Coincidence has a long arm but it is not an octopus. He thought he would sooner crash the car than be caught at this stage. He tried to snatch at the wheel.

"Leave it alone," grated Sarah through teeth that were clenched like rocks to prevent her trembling. "You'll wreck us all."

The big car climbed steadily from the valley below, making no more of the steep road than a child bowling a hoop along a sidewalk. The driver, who must now have perceived the black car racing like a demon along the road above, sounded his horn once more. Martin squeezed his. The noise was pandemonium.

"Stick to it," Martin told the girl. "We've right of way."

"It's no good," said Sarah. "You'll have to let him through." She put a foot on the brake. The big car floated up the hill, reached the upper road and ran around a corner. Martin heaved a deep sigh. He had feared it would block his path; now he was able to believe it had no concern with himself. In the darkness it had been impossible to make out any detail.

"Take your foot off the brake," he said, hissing. "You won't catch that car, not even if we go all out."

Sarah sailed around the corner—the car behind them was suddenly quiet again—then trod on the brake so sharply the car almost stood on its tail. A big olive-green car stood like a sort of graceful hippopotamus, square across the road. The driver opened the door and stepped out. The following car also turned and stopped. The driver extinguished his lights, then he in his turn stepped into the road. Quick as a flash Martin had dragged the girl from behind the wheel and now stood with his back to the hedge by the roadside, one arm folding Sarah closely to his chest, the other flourishing the gun so that both men could see it.

"One squeak out of either of you," he said, "and the girl gets it. And I don't mean maybe. Now then, you two, hands over your heads and keep them there."

"He means it," said Crook, putting up big freckled hands nearly as big as hams.

"You do like your drama done up in color," said the driver of the olive-green car, but he followed suit. "This isn't Madame Tussaud's waxworks."

"It better be, unless you want it turned into an auxiliary graveyard." Both men knew that Martin was capable of shooting all three of them out of sheer spite, and keeping the fourth bullet for himself. "Get forward," he ordered Crook, "up against the hedge." As Crook complied Martin turned his wrist in a lightning flash and put a bullet into one of the Superb's tires. The big car rocked for a moment; even Crook turned a shade pale.

"That's put you out of action," Martin said.

"It's also closed your own path of retreat," Crook pointed out.

"I don't happen to be going that way."

"How do you propose to get out then? You can't fly, and my friend's car's blocking the road ahead. There isn't an earthly chance you could get your rattletrap around him, and that lane he's backed into is a dead end."

"When I give the word he'll move his car," Martin said.

Crook opened his big eyes wide. "Why? He's on our side. And if you were thinking of using your next bullet on him," he added smartly, "my bet is he's got the ignition key in his pocket, and I don't think you'd fancy searching a dead man, not without me and Sugar was dead first, because it's bad policy to turn your back on an enemy, and Sugar and me have four hands between us."

Martin showed his teeth in an unpleasant grin. And very nice teeth, too, Crook reflected. Only you can say the same of a man-eating tiger.

"You couldn't do it," said Crook temperately. "Not with three of us at different points of the compass. One of us 'ud jump you. If you don't believe me, try it and see. Now, I've got a better idea. Let's parley. Mind you, we're only speakin' for ourselves; what the French police do about you is their affair. But remember, if you've shot it out with us, you won't have much artillery left for them. Here's my proposal. We're only here to get Miss Hollis. We don't aim to compete with the *gendarmerie*. Send her over to us and you can go to hell for all we care."

Martin laughed. It was a grating sound. "You think I'd trust you?"

"Have you any choice?"

"I'm surprised at you, anyway. Aiding and abetting. How about British justice?"

"This don't happen to be Britain, and French justice ain't our affair. Now, we're unarmed, so you send Sugar over to us. Oliver 'ull shift his car—won't you, Oliver—and you can be out of the country before they get you."

"Nothing doing," Martin said.

"Say you put your plan into action, how were you planning to reach the coast?" That was Oliver, asking because he really wanted to know. "If you were thinking of walking—you're probably farther off than you realize—you'd be bound to miss the tide . . ."

"That'll be enough from you," Martin told him.

"I don't think you've got the picture yet," Oliver persisted. "If that gun shifts again I drop the key I have in my hand—Crook was right, it's the ignition key of my car—and down it falls among the trees; the day of doom could dawn while you were on your knees trying to locate it. Sorry," he added to Crook, "your conversational style's contagious. Did I make myself clear?"

"Now I'll do some talking," Martin suggested. "Get back into that car, and you"—he waved the gun in Crook's direction—"you get in beside him. And don't lower your hands or you might find yourself directing business with one arm for the rest of your days. Then you, Abercrombie, back up that lane, then switch off the ignition and throw out the keys."

"Not good enough," Oliver objected.

"Oh, be your age," cried Crook. "It's the best we can hope for. All he wants is time, and with both our cars out of action he's got it."

Reluctantly Oliver got into the driving seat, Crook floundered in beside him, and the big car slowly backed.

"Don't have any funny ideas about suddenly treading on the accelerator," Martin warned him, "because the gun would go off before you could turn, and you'd have had all your work for nothing."

Oliver backed, switched off the engine. "Now the keys," said Martin impatiently.

It was Crook who snatched them from his companion's hand and tossed them through the window onto the road.

"Pick them up," Martin ordered the girl, and when she didn't instantly move he jabbed her savagely with the gun.

"I can't see them," she whispered, horrified to find tears pouring down her cheeks. She put up a hand to rub them away.

"More to the right, Sugar," called Crook. Sarah moved blindly forward, the gun following her smallest movement.

"Wanted, one miracle," announced Crook in clear tones. He was the only one of the four who was not surprised when he got one.

Sarah was groping in the dust, unable to locate the little key. The two men in the Panther were watching her like hawks when suddenly out of the dark came the blaring of a car horn.

Martin swung around in instinctive dismay only to find himself blinded by the headlights of the Superb that suddenly came on like the eyes of avenging angels. The door of the big yellow car opened, and something huge and dark like a malign spirit of the woods launched itself on the startled man. In the ensuing instant the gun clattered from his hand and a great foot kicked it out of reach. Arms taut as a noose came around his neck, jerking his head back till the spinal column was threatened; he could make no sound. Then he was assailed by what appeared to be about a ton of bricks from the other side, and that was Crook going into action. Oliver, seeing he was not really needed at this juncture, got out and found the car key.

"What's happened?" Sarah whispered. "I couldn't see it."

He coaxed her back into the Panther. "This is what's known as returning good for evil," he said.

"I thought you were dead." She wept, her last residue of courage melting away. "Why aren't you?"

"It's a long story," said Oliver soothingly. "I'll tell you later. In the meantime just mop up." He felt in his pocket and found a handkerchief. "I always thought it was local color, the hero giving the girl something to dry her eyes with, but that's another mistake I made." He looked out of the car window. Martin seemed to be lying on the ground with two heavy bodies pinning him down.

"There's some rope in my car," Crook said. "You might pass it out, and we'll make a good job of it."

"Who's your friend?" asked Oliver, doing as he was asked. "My God, it's the curé. How did he get here? On a celestial broomstick?"

"Nothing so elite. He traveled on the floor of my car, and very uncomfortable he must have been."

"Just you wait till your bishop hears about it," grunted

Martin. Oliver was slightly surprised to find he was still breathing. "I thought it was funny from the start, the way you chased around after the girl . . ."

"Watch it!" said Oliver. "I've got two feet, remember, and not just for standing on. Neither me nor Crook is an English gentleman, and we wouldn't mind roughing you up a bit. You might thank your stars the curé is here."

"Be quiet!" said the curé in a voice that staggered them all. "Do what you must, but remember—this is still a man."

"If you say so," agreed Oliver unrepentantly. "But I've had nicer specimens in cages when I was in the circus . . ."

He found the rope and they trussed Martin like a chicken. Oliver found a bottle in his pocket and passed it to Sarah. "We could all do with it, I should think," he said. "You take the first whack."

He and Crook changed the wheel of the Superb, thus taking care of the flat tire, while the curé joined Sarah in the Panther.

"I didn't mean to drag you into anything like this," she whispered to the priest. "It all blew up like the atom bomb."

He looked at her in open surprise. "I was there from the beginning," he told her. "This is one of my people."

He may be a wolf to us, she reflected, passing the bottle on, but to the curé Martin is still one of the sheep.

They left the black car drawn up against the hedge, none of them wanting to drive in a car the police were after. Crook went first into the driver's seat of the Superb, with the curé and Martin in the back. Oliver followed with Sarah.

"We'll stop at the first house we come to," Crook suggested, "and use a telephone. Let the police know they can call off their dogs, we're bringing home the bacon."

The first house, ironically, was Les Hirondelles, where a light still burned in a ground-floor window. The policeman, Michel, came to the door, obviously hoping this was his replacement, so that he might go home and sleep. When he saw Crook he stared.

"Borrow the lady's phone?" said Crook.

The light from the hall streamed through the open door and fell on the ignoble figure of Martin bundled in the corner of the car.

"What is this?" demanded Françoise, hurrying onto the path. She saw her lover and her face hardened. "Tell them I knew nothing of Mrs. Abercrombie's death," she said. "That, at least, you can do for me." She turned and walked back into the house.

It seemed to Sarah the night would never end. At the police station statements were taken, questions asked. Crook suggested, "Tomorrow is also a day," but the police had no mercy. When Martin had been taken away Oliver said abruptly, "You can't go back to the villa tonight, Sarah," and Crook rejoined, "She can come with me. If they haven't another room she can have mine. I'll share the garage with the Superb if need be. I can sleep anywhere. Oliver'll run the curé back, won't you, Oliver? Now, Sugar, if you've got any more questions you keep them for the morning. As it is, 'the night is far spent, the day is at hand.' And if Johnny turns up before midday they can put him to wait in the bar."

14

It was four o'clock next day before Sarah reappeared downstairs at the inn, in a pair of borrowed shoes, and by that time Johnny had been and gone. She got the message from Arthur Crook, who looked as fresh as paint and like the man who had had two tigers for breakfast.

"Gone?" she said in dismay.

"Came in to say good-bye, but I wouldn't let him disturb your beauty sleep. Had a letter from some friend of his in England that's followed him round for two or three days suggesting he should join up for a tour of Europe. I persuaded him to accept. That Johnny 'ull be a tycoon one of these days; knows when it's time to pull out and never look back. He left a note for you. Now, Sugar, take that glum look off your face. You know you didn't want him."

"I'd like to have seen him once more, though. He did a lot for me. As a matter of fact, I thought he'd be the one in your car last night instead of the curé."

Crook shook his big red head. "Too young. Too young for

patience, I mean. If we'd had Johnny with us last night we'd all have come back in boxes, the kind that are screwed down and never reopened. When that chap was manhandling you, Johnny wouldn't have contained himself; he'd have had all our names on the Roll of Honor. Now, Oliver . . ."

"I don't know what to say to him," muttered Sarah.

"Why not give him the surprise of his life and let him do the talking?"

"I don't even know his real name."

"You'll be able to ask him that, too. You'll be seeing him presently. I thought I'd just put you in the picture first. We've had quite a ball here this morning. They brought Marie in. If you ask me, Martin's lucky to be under lock and key. Give her half a chance and she'd be wearing his guts for garters. She's sold him down the river at bargain prices as it is."

"When she heard about Madame Auberon, I suppose. Mr. Crook, I can't forget that woman's face when she came out last night and saw Martin tied up like a parcel. All she could say was not to forget to let them know she wasn't concerned in Mrs. Abercrombie's murder. Because if he cared for anyone it was for her. He took a huge chance hanging about in the woods, waiting for a message even if she couldn't come, and she just sat tight and didn't lift a finger."

"You can't blame her, Sugar," said Crook. "He was a party to putting one woman underground and you'd have been the second. That kind of thing becomes a habit."

"He'd never have hurt her. It was his saving grace."

"Well, it ain't going to save him here," Crook assured her brutally. "Mind you, a lot will depend on what the jury likes to believe. According to Marie, it was him shot Mrs. A. The way he tells it, it was her picked up the gun."

Sarah shivered. "It seems so awful, to kill just for money. I suppose it was the treasure . . ."

Crook was looking unusually grave. "It was more than the diamonds—yes, that's the form the treasure took—and while Mrs. A. and later the police were hunting around for it, to say nothing of uninvited guests, the Ribauds knew just exactly where it was. It's funny, you know, you could have put your hand on it yourself any time after you got into his car. Still, we'll come to that."

"Diamonds?" repeated Sarah.

"Old man Abercrombie might be an Exclusive Saint, but he had all his wits about him. Well, he'd survived the wicked twenties, when all over the world money wasn't worth the paper it was printed on. But diamonds are forever. Who said that? And don't tell me James Bond. Like I said, it wasn't just the diamonds as money. To Martin and Marie they represented twenty years of servitude; it can't have been much of a party living at the villa. Just think, those two could never take a holiday or even go out together; always one of them had to be within call. But they consoled 'emselves with the thought that when the old girl handed in her chips they'd have the villa. It may not seem much of a place to you, but land and what stands on it is everything in *la belle France*. Mind you, I daresay they didn't expect the old lady to hold out so long. But there's no reason to suppose they did anything to assist her passage to the tomb. The lawyer warned them they couldn't think about taking possession till he'd explored every avenue; there was always a chance the missing brother had left an heir. And then out of the blue comes the widow from Paris, walks in as cool as you please, and treats them as if they were part of the furniture. No recognition for their years of service—they had ten thousand francs' legacy between them, and according to my reckoning that's about 750 pounds or 2,100 dollars in Oliver's currency. So you can't really blame them for keeping quiet about the diamonds. 'I shall let the villa for the summer,' says Mrs. A. 'I haven't time to make any other arrangements. I'm going on this yacht trip. When I come back I'll see about selling the house and property. You can stay on till then.' They might have been a couple of armchairs that were out-of-date. Why, she wasn't even going to let them keep that old car. Naturally the courts are going to call this murder, but to my mind it's next door to suicide."

"How did they find the treasure?" Sarah asked.

"A matter of luck, like so much in life. They'd rootled round everywhere till Marie realized that wherever the stuff was—and mind you, at that stage they'd no notion what shape it would take—it would be somewhere the old lady could keep an eye, if not a hand, on it. That cut out the shed, the garage, even the attics, because during that last year of her life she slept downstairs. She'd even had to give up goin' out to cash her own precious check, wrapped in the old fur coat . . ."

"I know," agreed Sarah. "Like a bear's pelt and nearly as heavy; only she didn't look like a bear, more like a shrew-mouse. She wore it all the year round—the curé told me." She stopped dead. "You don't mean that had anything to do with the treasure?"

"There were four fur buttons on the coat, about as big as tea plates. Well, the lawyer told the Ribauds they could sort the clothes. They weren't goin' to add to the value of the estate, and even Marie didn't see herself wearing that fur coat. Besides, the moths had been waiting a long time. Only, being a careful body, it occurred to her she might cut off the buttons, they might come in useful. Perhaps she heard something rattle, perhaps one of the buttons had got a few loose stitches. Anyway she opened them, and there were the diamonds. I ain't Bill Parsons—that's my partner and what he don't know about the ice ain't worth knowing—but I'd say there was plenty of stuff there. They could sell them abroad. What's more, they weren't hot, and there's plenty places where it's not thought politic to ask too many questions. Must have given them quite a tickle to see Madame going round banging on the walls or taking up the rugs looking for the treasure, because, according to Marie, she believed in it as much as anyone else.

"Well, then the chance came. Madame was going away, the villa was let, Martin and Marie for the first time in twenty years could get off together. The plan was they should come back the following week and guard Madame's valuable property while you were on the premises, but I don't think either of them ever considered that. They'd stay at Lourdes till Marie's grandchild was born; then they'd just vanish like smoke. By the time Madame came back from her cruise they could be the other side of the world.

"Anyway, that's what Marie thought. As we know, Martin had other ideas. It 'ud have been simple enough. He'd just take the car out one morning, slip back and collect his Françoise and remain missing for the duration. Came the last day, they were in a bit of a tizz I shouldn't wonder, and they couldn't resist pouring out the treasure on to the tabletop in the lodge and having a final gloat. I daresay Martin humored his wife, knowing this was the last time she'd clap her peepers on them.

"And then disaster, in the shape of Madame Abercrombie, strikes. Madame finds your telegram brought up with the milk or what have you and left by the door. It don't occur to her to put off her own trip or ask her minions if it 'ud be convenient for one of them to stop on; she sails down the path to tell them what she's decided. And she looks through the window and she sees the jewels. And, like a lot of dames when confronted with precious stones, she loses her head.

"What she should have done, of course, was creep back, get the police on the phone—the lawyer, too, if there was time—and then wait. Instead of which she goes storming in, tells them she knows what their honesty's worth and let's see what kind of a case they can put up in a court of law. Then when she sweeps out again, one of the Ribauds—I daresay we will never know which—picks up the gun and plugs her in the back. There's advantages in shooting down your victim in the open—no blood on the carpet, no mess—and then that night's rain would help them, too. Only now they've got to work and work fast. Madame's due to go to Pau, and to Pau she must be seen to go.

"I don't think they had any time for cold feet; there was too much to do. They drag Madame into the shed (I'd say), lock the door, Marie gets into Madame's coat and a hat no one else in St. Mariole would have been seen dead in, and off they go. Madame not only departs from Pau, she's seen to depart.

Then back comes Martin, runs across the curé in the village, volunteers the information that he's just driven Madame in, and back to the interment ceremonies. He took her down to the marsh in the wheelbarrow, of course. The ground 'ud be easier there, but even so, digging a grave is never child's play, and he's got to have everything shipshape for you tomorrow. But this changes his plans a bit. No question now of his going to Lourdes. He phones his girl friend—coast's clear, he says, come and help me straighten up a bit and we can be off tonight. They'd have left a note for you, I daresay, probably saying the wire arrived after Madame's departure, hope it won't be too inconvenient them being away, but everything's in order and be seeing you next week.

"And then you spoil everything by coming a day too soon. Naturally you mistake Madame Auberon for Mrs. A., but he don't see any harm—not till you let on you've seen the curé; and of course the curé knows it can't be Mrs. A. because she departed that morning. Martin knows, too, that if Marie rings up—and of course she will when her ever-loving don't arrive at Lourdes—she'll identify Anonyma and see which way the cat's jumping. All she's got to do is alert the police, spill the beans, putting all the blame on him—they could be stopped and arrested. And come to think of it, the life of one English miss don't seem a big price to pay, considering what's at stake, particularly if it can be made to look like an accident. Anyway, that's the decision he made. That sort of thing—murder, I mean—is always a gamble, and in his case it didn't come off. The trouble is, it's like a stone rolling downhill. Once it starts you can't stop it. And however far-sighted Martin was, he couldn't allow for Johnny and Oliver and me. Why, the dice were loaded against the fellow from the start."

"When I came over," said Sarah after a long pause, "Pat and Polly said they hoped I wouldn't find things too dull on my own."

"Hope is not yet taxed," Crook reminded her. "What are you proposing to do now? You won't want to go back to that mausoleum at St. Mariole."

Sarah looked surprised. "Why not? It's safe enough now.

And I can't disappoint Pat and Polly; they're simply counting on coming here."

Crook clutched his thick red thatch. "Sometimes I wonder if my share of purgatory will be to find myself a married man," he said. "The sex don't tick by any machinery we can understand. Here comes Oliver now," he added, in relieved tones. "I'll go and see the landlord about my bill. My job's through here now, and I had a call from Bill by long distance this morning that made my mouth water."

"Don't go," whispered Sarah. "Don't you want a drink or something?"

"And I know where to get it. I never did fancy myself as Monsieur de Trop, and there's an old English proverb about three bein' a crowd. Come right in, Oliver, and say your piece."

"They don't charge for sitting down," said Oliver, breaking a silence Sarah felt might go on forever. "I really came to bring you a pair of your shoes and this." He pulled an envelope out of his pocket. "Found it knocking about at the villa. They have a casual sort of way with their telegrams here."

"I don't know why anyone should be sending me telegrams," Sarah murmured, taking it. She read the message and lay back against the cushion of the hard little chair. "I wonder how long that's been there."

Oliver gently took the paper from her hand. "Polly down with mumps. Holiday off. Have fun. Pat," he read. "How careless of Polly."

"That settles Mr. Crook's question of what I'm going to do next. I shall go home, of course."

"Have you had mumps?"

Sarah considered. "I don't believe I have."

"I'd be delighted to offer you the hospitality of my home for so long as you care to enjoy it," said Oliver formally.

"Your . . . ? Oh, of course, the villa belongs to you now, I suppose, if you can convince the lawyer."

"I've got enough evidence to convince a whole bunch of

bishops. Now, Sarah, don't start asking more questions. We'll have plenty of time to mull it all over in the long evenings ahead. It can't be the first time a chap involved in a motor smash has gone to a hospital with the wrong label."

She thought a minute. "You mean someone else was buried as Oliver Abercrombie?"

"You catch on fast," Oliver congratulated her. "Still, I daresay that doesn't bother him much now. And I'm sure I don't grudge him the shelter of my name. I'm too pleased to find myself still alive."

She cried out, "I might have killed you."

"You did your best and, as Crook would say, an angel can do no more. Still, look on the bright side. If this incident proves to you that I'm practically indestructible . . ."

"Do you have to make a joke of everything?" she demanded fiercely. "Why do you suppose I didn't feel so badly about Martin as the rest of you? Because I felt I was on a par with him. He—or he and Marie between them—shot Mrs. Abercrombie because she was in the way. I didn't feel I was any better than he was."

The treacherous tears started again. "Go on," said Oliver unsympathetically, "enjoy yourself. The time might come when I shall find it an advantage to have a living fountain in my front garden."

"In your . . . ?"

"That's what I came about; the telegram was no more than my visiting card. Now listen, Sarah, and give your whole mind to what I'm saying. When they let me out of the hospital over there, and I was finally convinced who I was—I had a blackout that lasted for weeks—it seemed to me it might be a good idea to come over and sort of get myself established by looking up the home of my fathers. Before I landed I kept telling myself that bang on the head must have affected my judgment. Where was the sense in hunting out some ratty little hovel my father hated so much he couldn't even stay there? Still, I'd come a long way, so I finished the trip. And then the gate opened and you walked in. Crook is right, that a hunch is better than all the logic in the world. I knew then why I'd come halfway across the world and wasn't going back till I'd made a hundred percent effort to claim my inheritance, and I don't mean the villa. I realized it would be too much to expect you to have an immediate reaction . . ."

"Well, I should hope so," said Sarah. "I came on ahead of the others to nurse a ruptured heart. Simon . . ."

"The boy friend? Don't give him another thought, he's not worth it. Besides, these chaps that chop and change make the most indifferent husbands."

"That won't affect me," Sarah assured him dryly. "He's married to someone else."

"Serve him right. You've rented my villa for another three weeks, haven't you? That should give you time to come around to my way of thinking. Would you advise me to keep the villa?" he added. "Just as a pied-à-terre, say? Think it over."

He got up and went away. He came back presently with two large glasses, one of which he put into her hand. "I suppose you didn't think of having any food?"

"Mr. Crook did. He told them to bring me up a tray."

"Doesn't miss a trick, does he? What are you going to do when he goes back to London, which I gather he's on the point of doing?"

"I would like to go back to the villa," Sarah said. "I've hardly seen anything of it, and if it's going to stay in the family—I'll tell you one thing, Oliver. There's a frightful lot of junk there we shall have to get rid of. I saw the most enchanting little chest in a side street when I was marketing here . . ."

"Say good-bye to the young lady from me when she comes out of her trance," said the unchivalrous Mr. Crook to the landlord. "I'd have had a word with her myself, but she's pretty busy right now. Got any champagne? Oh well, it doesn't matter, give them whatever there is when the time comes. In the state they're in they won't know the difference."

"I knew she'd take him," he confided to the Superb as they started on their homeward run to the coast. "He's just the chap for her—boundless energy. Well, look at the way he's gone bouncing round the world. She'll enjoy that. Not like me. I'm a natural home bird."

He was visualizing Earl's Court on a Saturday night with about fourteen nations meeting and mingling, the lights up over The Two Chairmen, motors running, the planes overhead bringing holidaymakers home, the big gray and white coaches turning in at London's air terminal. He could hardly wait. "There's only one journey I really enjoy," he confessed aloud to himself, "and that's the long road home."

About the Author

ANTHONY GILBERT is the pseudonym for an English author who writes novels of contemporaneous English life and probably does not wish to confuse the authorship of those books with his murder mysteries. The name Anthony Gilbert has become synonymous with that of Mr. Crook, insouciant criminal lawyer, who has appeared as the *deus ex machina* in these tales of violence.